SAM CRESCENT

EVERNIGHT PUBLISHING ®

www.evernightpublishing.com

Copyright© 2020

Sam Crescent

Editor: Karyn White

Cover Artist: Jay Aheer

ISBN: 978-0-3695-0274-2

ALL RIGHTS RESERVED

SAM CRESCENT

MARRYING AN ASSHOLE

Dirty Fuckers MC, 3

Sam Crescent

Copyright © 2016

Prologue

Suzy knew she should ask Pixie to stop, but she couldn't say the words. What would be wrong with getting rid of her virginity once and for all? Pixie wasn't the kind of guy to care that it was her first time, nor would he want her to commit to him. This wasn't any kind of declaration or yearning for love.

Pixie, a member of the Dirty Fuckers MC, hadn't left her alone, nor had he taken no for an answer.

"Why me?" she asked, holding her hand up as he made to grab her.

"Why not you?" He reached down, gripping her ass, and moaning as he did. "Fuck, I love your ass. I love your body. I've never been a guy to love bigger women, but you're damn fine."

His touch didn't repulse her. Suzy wasn't rushing to get away from him, nor did she want him to leave.

What's the harm?

Why keep fighting?

"This doesn't mean anything?"

5

"It doesn't have to mean a damn thing." He sank his fingers into her hair and pulled her close. Her bra-covered tits crashed against his naked chest, and she whimpered.

Gripping his shoulders, she pulled him close to her, shoving his jacket off, and tearing at the shirt covering his chest. She didn't want anything else between them, and right now, he was wearing too many clothes.

"Where's your room?" he asked.

She pointed behind her, and gasped as he lifted her up.

There's no point in telling him about my little virgin problem. He won't notice.

Suzy giggled as he dropped her to the bed. He stepped away, his hands going to the belt of his jeans.

"Take your clothes off, baby. I want you completely naked when I fuck you."

She pushed her jogger pants down her thighs as Pixie revealed his dick. For a second she could only stare. He was huge. It wasn't normal. Maybe she needed glasses, and it was just a trick of the light.

"Um, is that normal, or do you have a cover over it or something?"

He chuckled. "I can tell you, you've never had a man as big as me."

I've never had a man at all.

It couldn't be that bad.

Women did it all the time.

Sometimes it hurt, and other times it didn't.

Flicking the catch at the back of her bra, she peeled it down her arms, and finally stood before him naked. Licking her dry lips, she smiled at him.

"I'm here."

He stepped up to her, wrapped his arms around

her back, and drew her close. "I've spent so many hours thinking about what I'd do to you once I got you here."

"And now?"

"I'm going to do every single dirty thing I can in the time I'm here."

She pressed her thighs together, feeling the heat blooming within her pussy. It was wrong of her, but she wanted him. Damn, did she want him. Months of denying herself, and she couldn't wait another second.

Sinking her fingers into his hair, which he'd been growing out lately, she pulled him down toward her. Claiming his lips, she moaned as he plundered her mouth with his tongue, deepening the kiss.

"This first time is not going to be slow. I've wanted you too damn long, and I don't know how long I'm going to be able to last." He pushed her to the bed, and she tucked some hair behind her ears as she watched him grab a condom.

It was really going to happen.

Even as she was excited about having sex for the first time, there was also a little fear.

Taking a deep breath, she moved back on the bed until she was lying against the pillows.

Pixie climbed onto the bed, spreading her thighs. He didn't come up over her. He paused at her pussy, and she looked down in time to see him open the lips of her sex, and then swipe his tongue from her clit down.

She cried out, the pleasure going from zero to a million within a tiny second. All it had taken was the touch of his tongue, and she loved it. He didn't stop there. He sucked, licked, and flicked at her clit, each new touch sending her hurtling even further into pleasure. She had touched herself. There was no chance in hell of her staying a virgin without touching herself. She hadn't used dildos or vibrators as she had wanted that first time to mean something.

Right that second, she truly believed waiting for that special someone was overrated.

Pixie was showing how many women he'd been with, and also how good he'd gotten at pleasuring women.

"You taste so fucking good, baby," he said against her pussy.

"Please, Pixie." She didn't have a clue what she was asking him for.

The fire burning inside her needed putting out, and the only person who could do that was the man between her thighs.

"Fuck, I want to feel you come all around my dick."

He moved from between her thighs, and then she felt the hard press of his dick against her entrance.

"You've got a condom on, right? I'm not protected." She'd always been regular with her periods, so she'd never felt the need to go on the pill. Also, no boyfriend, no sex, no risk of pregnancy or STDs, or STIs. No wonder she'd stayed a virgin for so long.

Having sex was a walking, talking disaster.

"I've got my dick bagged. Don't worry. I don't want any brats running around. That's not the way I roll."

"You know you're an asshole, right?"

"I never said I wasn't."

He kissed her, silencing any more of her protests, which only served to annoy her even more.

"You can't kiss me to keep me quiet!"

"But it works so well."

He claimed her lips once again, and this time, the tip of his cock pressed to her entrance, and kept on going.

Suzy tensed up as the pressure became almost

unbearable. Within a second, the pain was white-hot between her thighs, making her tears well. Instead of pushing him away, she gripped him tighter, trying not to show how painful it was. She never expected the searing pain, or the panic that suddenly consumed her.

"You're so fucking tight." He growled the words against her throat.

Squeezing her eyes tightly shut, her entire body tensed up.

Seconds passed, maybe even minutes, and then she heard him, and realized that Pixie hadn't moved at all.

"What's wrong?" he asked, pushing hair out of her face.

"Nothing." It was so much easier to lie than to tell the truth.

"You don't think I can't feel the change in you. You're all tense, and it's not in a good way."

"It's fine. Just, you know ... finish."

He frowned, staring down at her. She hated how he kept looking at her, almost as if he was seeing something that she really didn't want him to see.

"Suzy, babe, are you a virgin?" he asked.

"No. I'm not."

"You're lying."

"I'm not."

"Then look me in the eyes and say you're not."

She looked up at him, and for some strange reason couldn't bring herself to say the words.

"You're a virgin?"

"Yes." The word escaped her on a whisper.

"Why didn't you say anything?"

"And have you laughing at me?"

"I'm not laughing."

She glared at him. "Fine! Why aren't you

laughing?"

"I don't think this is funny. I'm an asshole, Suzy, but I want you to want this."

"I do." She gave a little wiggle, biting her lip, expecting pain. Nothing happened. "It doesn't hurt."

"It hurts for women, but if the guy you're with knows this, he knows to take it slow, and to make sure she has time to get accustomed to his dick inside her."

"I'm completely confused with the tenses you've just used."

"Me too. Anyway, you should have told me. I could have made this a lot better for you."

"How?"

"Simple, I could have at least distracted you with an orgasm."

"Oh."

"Yeah, oh." He stroked her cheek, and then fanned her hair out onto the pillow.

"Can you still make it good for me?" she asked.

"That depends."

"On what?"

"Give me complete and total submission to do what I want to you, every time we're together, and I'll make it good for you."

"Pixie, it's only going to be this one time."

"Or any time the need takes us."

She rolled her eyes. There was no way they were going to be going for a second time. This was a one-time deal. She didn't need her friends thinking she was weak. None of them liked Pixie. *She* didn't like him half the time. He was an arrogant ass.

"Deal."

"Good girl."

He pulled away from her but not out of her.

She stared up as he ran his gaze all over her body.

His hands went to her breasts, cupping them. "I really do love your big tits. So full, round, and begging to be fucked." He pressed them together and gave a little moan. "My cock would fit perfectly here." He ran his fingers through the valley of her tits before stroking her nipples. She arched up, gasping as pleasure rushed through her body, going straight to her clit. "I feel how much you like that. Your tits are sensitive."

"Is that a good thing?"

"Some women don't have much in the way of sensation when it comes to their tits. I'd say it's a good thing."

"Don't talk about other women!"

"Feeling a little jealous?"

"How would you feel if I talked about other men?"

"Babe, we both know you haven't been with other men."

"Doesn't stop me from finding them attractive, and right now, any guy is looking better."

He winced. "Oh, you sting me."

She cried out as he pinched her nipple then leaned down, sucking the bud into his mouth. Gripping the bed sheet beneath her, she cried out, shocked by how instant the arousal was.

"You've got no idea how many tricks I've got up my sleeve. I can have you panting, and begging for it for days."

"It sounds to me you're all about the talk, Pixie. Why don't you prove it?"

He sat back once again, and a second later she felt his thumb against her clit. "I'll prove it, all right. First I want you to come all over my cock, and then I'll fuck you until the only name you remember is mine."

She wrapped her legs around his back, moaning

as he teased her clit. He didn't release her, not until she screamed his name as her first orgasm at a man's hand rushed through her. It was stronger, better, and more intense than any she'd found herself. She also loved the feel of his rock hard cock inside her.

Pixie moved back over her, grabbed her hands, and locking them either side of her head. "Now the real fun can begin."

He pulled out of her so only the tip of his cock was inside, the slammed every inch of him within her.

She screamed his name as he rode her body hard, forcing her to take every single inch, and then more, drawing a second orgasm out of her as he rode to the first.

When it was over, she was shocked by how quickly he disappeared.

Suzy lay on the bed, feeling a little torn.

Glancing over at the clock, she saw that within fifteen minutes he'd completely shattered her world, leaving her open and exposed. Tears filled her eyes. She was expecting him to leave, but instead he came back to bed with a cloth.

"I noticed a little blood on my dick when I played with your pussy." He wiped the cloth between her thighs, and she stared at him, somewhat touched by his caring act. Out of all of the men at the Dirty Fuckers MC, Pixie was the most selfish bastard she had ever met.

Licking her dry lips, she swallowed the lump and forced herself to stare at him.

"I'm not a total asshole, Suzy."

He wiped her clean, and even though she was mortified, she didn't push him away. Her heart was racing as he helped her.

"One night, right?" she asked, making sure she didn't read too much into it.

"One night."

This she could handle without getting her heart broken. Pixie was the kind of guy to break women's hearts. She didn't want to have to deal with that kind of pain.

She hoped she never would.

****

"Oh, God, yes, yes," Suzy said, moaning.

"Not God, baby. It's me." Pixie slammed back inside her, making her scream his name once again. She couldn't deny him, nor did she want to. Right now they were in her workplace, in the backroom at the desk where Pixie was fucking her so damn good. One time had turned into two, then three, and now she found it impossible to fight off her need for him.

"Touch your pussy, Suzy. Make yourself come just like I know you can."

Reaching between them, she stroked over her clit, gasping with each press of his cock inside her. His body pushing her finger against her clit was such a delicious friction.

Suddenly, he pulled out, and Suzy watched as he shoved her hands aside, taking her clit into his mouth, sucking on the bud.

"What are you doing?" she cried out.

He flicked her clit, sliding down to plunge inside her. Pixie was an inventive lover, and he hadn't grown tired of her. It had been a couple of months since he'd taken her virginity, and instead of them separating, they always found their way back to each other.

"I'm never going to get tired of your pussy. So fucking perfect, and never been touched by another man." He licked inside her several times. "So tasty."

Heat filled her face as he continued to lick and suck at her clit. Pixie always went down on her. It was like he couldn't get enough.

Gripping the edge of the desk, she watched as he teased her clit, staring up at her.

"Come for me, Suzy."

She let out a cry as he sucked her clit, hurtling her into an explosive orgasm that took her breath away.

"That's it, baby, give it to me." His thumb stroked over her clit, prolonging her orgasm.

Within seconds, he thrust inside her, and she whimpered at the sudden invasion.

"I love feeling you come," he said, slamming all the way within her.

He started to fuck her so that the desk began to move, which only stopped when he hit the wall.

"I love fucking you," he said.

She loved it when he did. There hadn't been anyone else, and she wasn't interested in finding anyone else either. The only person she craved was standing between her thighs, fucking her.

Pixie cupped her waist, his fingers digging into her hips as he spilled his arousal in the condom. She wouldn't allow him to go bareback as she didn't want to get on the pill. None of her friends knew she was having sex with Pixie, and so far she'd been able to keep it silent.

They didn't go on dates. He came by the apartment when Chloe was out. Seeing as Grace had moved in with Drake, it was only the two of them now.

She was panting along with him as reality set in.

Closing the shop was not good, and with their secret relationship it was starting to become a regular occurrence.

"You need to go," she said, still holding onto the desk as he rested between her thighs.

"Ah, so you've had your fun, and now it's time to

kick the boyfriend out."

"You're not a boyfriend, Pixie. Don't worry, I'd never mistake you for something like that. I shouldn't be closing the shop. We need all the sales we can get." She had been told that the shop was currently under threat, and might in fact close. Competition in the mall was fierce, and they just couldn't keep up.

Suzy didn't do anything other than sell, and help customers when she could.

"Why? What's going on?"

"It's nothing. Don't worry about it."

She winced as he pulled out of her. Suzy didn't want him remove the condom, or tie it up. "Is the shop in trouble?"

"I don't know. We can't keep having sex here."

"We could just go back to your place."

She shook her head.

Pixie sighed. "You do know our friends are going to know about us."

Shoving her skirt back into place, she bent down to grab her panties, and found them torn. "Seriously, why can't you wait for me to remove them?"

"I don't like you wearing panties. They get in my way."

"You're costing me a fortune replacing them."

"Don't replace them. I'll only keep tearing them off you."

"Yeah, and when you move on I won't have any panties left."

There was a pause.

"What makes you think I'm going to move on?"

"Isn't that what you do? Get bored, and move on to the next woman that you want."

"I'm not that cold-hearted. Besides, I've never cheated on a woman. I've never screwed a woman over."

Tucking her hair back into a ponytail, she was together enough to deal with him. Pixie was a strange man, one she'd truly thought she'd known. The more time she spent with him, the harder it was to put him into a category.

"I heard what you did to Cora. She told me how you, um, you arranged for your brother to be there to screw her as you don't like dealing with females who get attached to you."

He let out a string of curses. "Look, I'm a fucking asshole."

She held her hands up. "I think we're clear on that fact you can be one, yes."

Pixie closed the distance between them, wrapping his arms around her. "Even when I was chasing women, I didn't offer them anything, or make promises. I'm not that kind of guy."

She stared at his chest as her heart started to beat faster.

He's a player.

Licking her lips, she smiled. "There're no worries here, Pixie. You don't need to worry about anything."

"What's going on inside that head of yours?" he asked.

"Not a lot, but I've got to go to work if I want to keep a job."

He cupped her cheek, running his thumb across her bottom lip. "When can I see you again?"

"This was only supposed to be a one-time deal."

"So now it's a ten-time deal."

"I don't know." Pulling out of his arms, she took a step away. "I've got to work."

****

Pixie pushed Suzy down onto his bed within the clubhouse. Everyone else was around or in their room celebrating, and he wanted his woman all to himself.

"Do you trust me?" he asked.

"A little bit."

He pulled the cuffs from each corner of his bed, letting her see. "Enough to let me have you at my mercy?"

She licked her lips, and he noticed she did that whenever she was a little nervous. "You won't hurt me?"

"Never."

"Then yes, I trust you."

He sighed. It would do for now. Over the years he'd built himself up a reputation, and now he had to deal with the consequences.

Suzy was different from all of the women he'd fucked. For starters, he actually wanted her to like him. Never had he felt that experience before. He hated it when she always expected the worst, but again, it was what he deserved.

Securing one wrist, and then the other, he grabbed her scarf, and placed it over her eyes.

"Um, I didn't agree to this."

"Trust me." He pressed a kiss against the corner of her lips. Staring down at her freely, Pixie didn't hide his feelings from her. The way she made him feel, the passion, the need—all of it he allowed to show.

He had no doubt that if he even told her what he felt for her, she'd run. Suzy was scared, and she wouldn't even be seen with him in any other way than potential frenemies.

She licked her lips, and he stroked his hands down over her breasts, circling her nipples and moving down her body. Opening her thighs, he slid a finger between her wet pussy lips, teasing her clit. She let out a gasp.

"You're always wet for me."

"Pixie," she said, moaning.

"Tell me what you want."

"I want you."

"You'll get all of me."

Grabbing the condom, he tore into the packet, and slid the latex over his dick. He wasn't in the mood for taking his time today. At any time, they could be called out by either of their friends, and he wasn't willing to risk getting caught. Not today.

Placing his dick at her entrance, he slammed all the way inside, going to the hilt. They both cried out, and Pixie leaned over her, claiming her lips. He didn't remove the blindfold. Just this once, he wanted to own every part of her without holding anything back.

"This was never going to be a one-time deal." He understood that now more than ever.

"You'll grow bored soon."

He wouldn't argue with her. She'd see in time that he wasn't joking around. Slamming deep within her, Pixie claimed and owned her in equal measure. It was the way it was always going to be between them, and he didn't see a reason for it to stop now.

Soon they would be found out by their friends. Pixie only hoped that when that happened, she would have enough feelings for him not to call it a day.

Chapter One

Ten months later

Suzy had the worst luck in the world. Her job at the clothing store had come to an end as the company had gone under, and now she was heading home to trawl her way through the local newspaper. This was not what she wanted to have to deal with right now. She had no job, and Greater Falls didn't have many of those. After being handed her last week's pay, she'd walked around the mall hoping to find something to quickly transfer to. There was nothing. She either had no qualifications, or too many.

Entering her apartment, she smiled as Fluffy rushed toward her. The little Pomeranian was no longer a puppy, but he was so adorably small.

"Hey, little guy." She bent down, picking him up. "Did you miss me today?"

"Of course he did."

Suzy gasped, and turned to find Pixie coming out of her room. "What the hell? What are you doing here?"

"I wanted to meet you from work."

"You know Chloe lives here as well, right? That Grace also has a key to check on Fluffy."

"Yeah, yeah I know. I also know that Chloe is spending the weekend with Richard, and Grace is busy with her and Drake's baby. So I thought I'd come and check on your dog."

She let out a breath. "How did you even get in?"

He held up a set of keys.

"I didn't give them to you."

"No, you didn't, but I may have taken Grace's set, gotten them copied, and put the original key back before she knew."

She shook her head, not wanting to deal with this

right now. "Why am I not surprised?"

"Why are you home?" he asked.

"You're in my apartment, and you're asking me why I'm here?"

"It's the middle of the day. You don't usually get home 'til late."

"Yeah, well, I may have to actually have to move or something."

"Move where?"

"Out of Greater Falls," she said.

"This is a joke, right?"

"Nope. No joke. I wish it was. The shop closed down today. Ceased trading, and it was completely done." Even as she spoke, tears filled her eyes. Turning her back on him, she pressed her fingers against the bridge of her nose, begging for the tears to go.

He gripped his shoulders. "It's going to be okay."

"No, it's not. I don't have a job. This place is paid up for two months, that's it, and then I'm out of here. Crap, I better warn Chloe, but I don't want to worry her. She's taking it steady with Richard."

"Even though they're away together?"

"I don't judge. She's my friend."

He rubbed her shoulders. "We'll think of something."

Pulling out of his arms, she turned toward him, finally feeling like she could handle him. "Don't worry about it. I'll always figure something out."

She walked past him, heading toward her room. She put Fluffy down on the sofa on her way past.

"You don't have to do this alone."

"It's fine, Pixie. Honestly, getting a job is hard, but I tend to be good at whatever I do." Even with her size she'd been able to sell clothes to anyone. Sure, she'd had some really shitty customers who'd told her to lose some weight, and a few managers who thought her weight was a problem.

Running fingers through her hair, she stared at her room.

She truly was at a loss.

"This is what you mentioned a few months back, right?"

"Yeah. The shop has been struggling for months. I was hoping it was just a little slump. You know how the news talks about the markets, and confidence, and stuff. No such luck for me. I'm officially unemployed."

She pulled her shirt over her head, and grabbed a plain old red shirt that hung from her frame.

"I'm afraid I'm not going to be able to enjoy a quickie with you if that's what you were hoping for." She turned to face him, pulling her hair back into a ponytail. He leaned against her wardrobe, holding the pair of jeans she wanted. They were her comfy, doing-work jeans. "Thanks."

"I'm not just around for a quickie, Suzy. Besides, I was here to help Fluffy. I didn't know your job was going to be ending today."

"What were you doing in my room?" she asked. She wasn't accusing him of anything. Many nights she'd gone to bed to find him already in her apartment. She should probably be scared at how easy it was for him to get in and out of her room.

"I got you a little surprise, but I figure we'll use it another time."

"Okay." She wriggled out of her skirt and tugged her jeans up. "Do you know if Teri's hiring?"

"I don't think so. Grace is working for her."

She nodded. It would be too much luck for her to actually get a job with someone she wanted to work for. Teri worked for the Dirty Fuckers MC, but the truth was the woman owned the diner.

"It doesn't matter. I'll think of something."

Once she was dressed, she grabbed Fluffy and gave him a quick cuddle.

"Why don't you work for me?"

"Doing what?"

"I don't know. Screwing me."

"I'm not a whore, Pixie, but I appreciate you thinking of it." She smiled at him, knowing deep down that he was only trying to help.

There were rare moments during their time together that Pixie really did show another side to his personality. It was a side she truly believed she could fall in love with.

He stroked her cheek. "I'm here whenever you need me."

Following him out of her apartment, she snagged her jacket, and headed downstairs, wondering how he'd gotten to her apartment.

"Did you come by car or bike?" she asked.

"I walked."

"Wow, you walked all the way from the clubhouse?"

"Pretty much. I was stopping in to see James and Cora anyway."

Wrapping herself up, she felt the bitter chill of fall air. "It's not going to be long until winter is upon us, and snow."

"You can't be moving in winter."

"I'll do what I have to do."

"When can I see you again?"

"You come to my room every single night."

"I want a weekend."

She frowned. In the past ten months neither of them had moved their relationship from quick sex. Suzy had been too afraid of getting laughed at.

"I don't know, Pixie. This was supposed to be a one-time deal, remember."

"I remember everything, Suzy. We went past one time, one night, and we're in the hundreds, easily."

Staring up and down the street, she frowned. "I really don't know if we should do the whole weekend thing."

"You're always putting me off."

"And you're always trying to put me into a girlfriend category. You don't need to do that with me. I'm a sure thing."

When he made to touch her, Suzy didn't want to step back. Their relationship was based on sex, nothing else. Someone could see them at any moment, and yet, she couldn't care about anything but him.

"I'll be by tonight."

"We'll have the whole place to ourselves," she said.

"It's why I've got that little surprise. I'll bring dinner. Don't worry about cooking." He pressed a kiss to her lips, and she watched as he walked away.

Her lips felt swollen from his lips.

Get over it. He'll move on soon. Don't let your heart get involved.

She walked in the opposite direction for town. She stopped at the grocery store, picking up the local newspapers, and of course some of the city ones.

Pulling out her cell phone, she sent a text to Chloe, letting her know what had happened. She didn't expect to hear from the other woman yet.

Suzy walked around town, checking signs in windows just to see if something was there. She had grown up in Greater Falls, and it was where she'd imagined she'd stay.

Then she thought about Pixie. The club had been in Greater Falls for nearly seven years. She'd been finishing up the last year of high school when they arrived, and she'd avoided them. Until one day, two or three of them—she couldn't remember how many—had come to where she worked. The men had been with a couple of women, and Pixie had been there. It was her first time of seeing him, and it hadn't been her last. He'd always come into the shop, trying to talk to her, draw her into a conversation.

There were moments when he seemed determined to say the most disgusting and vulgar thing.

She would listen, and judge him, and then he'd leave.

Those times where Pixie showed up, she started to love, and to enjoy. His somewhat sexist comments, she started to find funny. He was a unique guy that took some getting used to, but when she finally did, he was actually nice.

Pushing her complicated feelings and thoughts about Pixie aside, she focused on the paper in hand. She needed to find a job, so, heading to the park, she took a seat, and started to look through the advertisements.

It didn't look good.

****

Pixie made his way back toward the diner, which wasn't far from the clubhouse. If he was going to find anyone to help give Suzy a job, it was going to be his brother and the club. They could find something for her to do, and he hadn't been kidding about paying her to screw him. Well, it wouldn't be like treating her like a whore. That wasn't what he meant. Men, husbands, boyfriends, they took care of their women and sex was involved. That was what he meant by doing it that way. She'd have to stay with him, and he'd officially get a key into her life. Everything he'd done so far had been in secret.

Entering the diner, the scent of the food made his mouth water, and he saw several of his club brothers sitting at a bunch of tables. Also, he saw Teri sitting between Leo and Paul, laughing.

This was his family, and also James was there, his real brother.

"Where you been?" Damon asked, making everyone turn toward him.

"Busy. Teri, I wanted to talk to you about something." He grabbed a chair, spun it around, and straddled the seat.

"Oh, I'm feeling all special now." Teri gave a wiggle and leaned forward, focusing on him.

"It's simple. Suzy needs a job, and I'm hoping you have one for her."

"Why does she need a job? Did you lose her the one she has by being yourself?" Teri asked.

"No. From what I can tell the business was having trouble, and they've gone under. Today they handed Suzy in her last pay, and that was it."

"Wow, she never said anything," Cora said. "Neither did Grace and Chloe."

"I like her," Kitty said. "She's such a sweet woman, and I doubt she'd worry anyone."

"They live with her though," Teri said.

"I know, but Chloe's away, and she's been struggling with her relationship with Richard. Then Grace has given birth to Joseph, and lives with Drake." Kitty shrugged. "Suzy wouldn't try to worry her friends."

"Shit, I'm really sorry, but I don't have any openings," Teri said.

"What about Grace's job? She's on maternity leave, right?"

"I've already replaced her for the time being, Pixie. Suzy should have come to me immediately."

"Fuck." He turned to his brother. "What about at the club?"

"She isn't part of the club, Pixie. You know I can't have her there."

"Ugh, just say she's mine, okay. She's my woman, and she can be at the club, serving some beers, or cleaning."

He saw his brother staring at him. James folded his arms, and kept on staring. Pixie hated it. His brother always saw shit he shouldn't.

"What's going on, Pixie? No bullshit."

"Fine. Suzy is a friend of the club women, and I want to help her."

"And if we don't?"

Pixie gritted his teeth, and he was ready to punch his own brother. "Then Suzy will have no choice but to head to the city, and she's already talked about leaving, and going there." He didn't like the pain that pierced him because of her leaving. It was simple to him. She wasn't ever going to leave, never ever. He didn't care how childish he sounded, it wasn't going to happen.

"How did you know all of this?" James asked.

"I was at her apartment. You know me. Still trying to get into her pants, and I thought being nice to her dog, she'd be more than willing to screw me." It wasn't a complete lie.

James smirked. "Right."

"What are you going to do?" Cora asked.

"Well, if I don't help, Pixie will throw one of his universally famous tantrums."

"He's a baby, we all get it."

"Yeah, but we have to live with him, and believe me when I say that he will find a way of making my life a misery." James ran fingers through his hair. Cora and James were partners in life. They were the first couple to settle down within the club. They were different because Cora didn't want to get married. It didn't mean they weren't in love. His brother and sister-in-law didn't need the world to know they were together.

They were strong.

James got up, and Pixie followed him out of the diner.

"What's really going on? And don't even think of getting smart with me. I'm not in the mood. You're acting like a girl, and what's worse, you're acting like an asshole, and you know I'm not in the mood to deal with your tantrums."

Pixie pulled a packet of cigarettes out of his jacket, and took one out, lighting it up. He offered one to James, who shook his head.

"Cora doesn't like my breath if I'm smoking, and she won't kiss me."

Pixie didn't question him.

Since being with Suzy he understood everything about accommodating what their women wanted. The thought of her not kissing him would stop him from smoking as well.

"Suzy's a great worker. She's hard-working. She's funny, and the guys would love her."

"This has nothing to do with getting in her pants?"

"No." He'd already gotten into those, but he wasn't about to tell his brother that. "I want to help her."

"You never help anyone."

"Well, I'm changing now. I want to help Suzy. If I don't, at the end of the month she's gone. I don't want that to happen."

James kept on staring at him. "I've never seen

you like this, Pixie. Not in the whole time since we've moved here, and certainly not before. You go through women faster than anyone at the club. I was the one who used to have to deal with your messes, remember?"

He'd always shared with his brother so that he could leave after fucking the woman senseless. In all of his life he'd never dealt with drama, and refused to even allow women to get attached to him.

The first time Pixie had seen Cora he had the same idea. It just so happened Cora had a spine, and told him to pretty much go get fucked. Not long after that he found Suzy, and the tempting little redhead wouldn't leave him alone. Of course it had been one sided. He wanted her, not the other way around. Suzy did nothing but try to push him away.

Now there was no turning back. No pretending for him.

One time hadn't been enough.

At first he'd thought it was because she was a virgin. Completely innocent, waiting for a guiding hand. Then his thoughts changed. It wasn't just about being the only man she'd ever been with. He'd wanted her, couldn't stop thinking about her. It only got more and more intense.

No other woman tempted him. He hadn't even tried to be with other women. Sure, the club whores and the local women had tried. He had a reputation, but he simply brushed them off. For the first time in his life, he was content.

Even when he was watching a movie with Suzy, he was at peace. He was used to the restless feeling, and the need to move on. That was no longer happening to him.

"Suzy is different, okay? If she leaves then I know I'm going to have a hard time dealing with my 'temper tantrum', as you call it. Please, give her a job, for me. I'll be there at the bar, or wherever you want her to work."

James held his hand up. "She won't need a babysitter. I'll go and see her this afternoon."

"You will?"

"Of course. She's a friend of Cora's as well. I'm not just going to let her leave."

"Thanks, James."

Pixie pulled him into a hug, and slapped him on the back.

"The women are talking about you," James said.

"What do you mean?"

"You're not up to your usual standard of sex. In fact, you're not sleeping with anyone, period."

"I decided to give myself a break."

"A break?"

"Yeah, I was getting bored with the same old holes, and I figured if I waited, they might seem new again." There, that was something an asshole would say.

James shook his head. "You wonder why the women don't want to stay around you."

"They only want to ride my dick."

"One day you will see there is more to life than getting your dick wet."

"Sure, sure. Marriage?"

"You don't need to be married to be content. Look at Cora and me. We're happy."

Pixie nodded. "Some people can't have that level of happiness." It was lies. He was doing this for Suzy. She didn't want anyone to know they were together. "Let me know what she says."

"Will do."

Pixie turned away and started walking back to the clubhouse.

All the time he was aware of James staring at him, and when he turned to give a wave, he was right. His brother was watching him intently.

Chapter Two

"Something is going on with Pixie," James said, parking his bike a few feet away from Suzy's apartment building. The moment he'd stopped his bike, he'd put a call through to his woman, needing to talk to her.

"Like what? He's an asshole most of the time," Cora said.

"I don't know. Something doesn't sit right with me with this one. He's an asshole to everyone, but with Suzy, he's trying to make it work."

"So he can sleep with her. She leaves, he's failed."

James stared up at the building, and rubbed his head. "This is different." He was the only one who really knew his brother. Sure, the women could all say they knew Pixie, but most of them didn't know his real name, Leonard, which he hated. "You know I've told you about him. I've always looked out for him."

"What are you going to do?"

"I'm going to offer Suzy a job. She'll be working closely with me. Can you handle that?"

"Handle what?"

"Me, working with a pretty woman, in my office."

Cora laughed. "Sweetie, are you trying to make me jealous?"

"Kind of. I love it when women are all over me, and you come doing your tiger routine, growling to get them away. You fuck my dick really well after that." He could see in his mind as she rolled her eyes.

"Suzy is a sweet woman. She'd never screw another woman's man. You've got more chance of getting a handjob from a monkey than getting anything from her. Besides, save yourself for me, and I can

31

promise you, you'll love it."

His dick was already getting hard. James would never stray, and neither would Cora. They weren't married, but they didn't need a slip of paper to remind them of their commitment. He loved her more than anything in the world. He refused to live without her.

"I've got to go. We'll chat when I get back."

"I'll be waiting for you, baby."

They hung up, and he made his way inside, up the stairs toward Suzy's apartment. Chloe, one of the women who used to be a club whore, lived with her. He stood outside Suzy's door, and wondered why the hell he was doing this. His brother was known for being difficult. James couldn't deny that he'd noticed a change in his brother over the past few months.

Everyone had been changing. Leo and Paul had finally moved on from their heartbreak over Stacey.

Knocking the door, he waited. Something was going on with Pixie, and he intended to find out.

"James, what are you doing here?" Suzy asked once she opened the door.

"I've got a proposition for you. Can I come in?"

"Of course, of course." She stepped away from the door, and allowed him to enter. "Are you sure you're looking for me?"

"Yeah, you're the only one that can help me."

He watched as she frowned before closing the door.

"How is Cora?" Suzy asked.

"She's good. Everyone is good. So, you've got no job and I'm here to offer you one."

"Just like that? Wait, how do you even know?"

"Pixie."

"Oh."

He watched as her cheeks heated, and she started

to move from side to side.

"Is everything okay?"

"Everything is fine." She moved toward the kitchen, and he followed her, taking a seat at the table. "What job could possibly be available? I've looked all over the town." She passed him over the paper. "And there's not a lot in there. I'm thinking I'm going to have to start looking for some other place to live. I'm not looking forward to telling Chloe."

James stared at her for several seconds. He didn't know exactly what was going on, but something was between this woman and Pixie. "You won't have to. You used management and accounting skills at your last job right?"

"Yeah. I took a class in college."

"Excellent. If you agree, I'll match whatever that fashion shop was paying, and increase it by five thousand. That way you won't have to move anywhere."

"Wow, seriously?"

"The catch is you'll be working in my office within the club. Anything and everything you see there is strictly confidential. You can't tell anyone."

"I won't. I promise." Her hands were pressed together, and she looked ready to squeal in excitement.

"I have one condition."

"Name it." She poured them both a coffee, and placed one in front of him.

"I want to know what is going on between you and Pixie. No bullshit. No lies."

She tensed up, licking her lips, and averting her gaze, which he found interesting.

When she went to open her mouth, he held his hand up. "I'd think twice about lying to me. It's one of the many things I can't stand."

"I don't really know what to say."

"The truth."

Suzy let out a breath. "We, um, I don't know if you'd call it seeing each other, or not."

"Are you dating?" How old was he? God, he felt like Pixie's damn father rather than his brother.

"No. We haven't been on any dates. We connected." She rubbed at her temple. "I don't feel comfortable telling you without Pixie being here."

"Something has happened."

"We slept together," Suzy said. "It was supposed to be one time, and it hasn't stayed one time."

"How long?"

Her gaze went past his shoulder, and he saw her working it out. "Nearly a year, I think."

"You're not pregnant."

"No, of course not. We're careful, and wear protection."

James smiled. "I wouldn't mind having a little nephew running around."

Suzy paled. "I don't want to have any kids."

"You don't?"

"Not yet, not now, and I don't think Pixie is the kind of guy you rely on for that."

"Wow, I think you underestimate Pixie."

"He passes responsibility on faster than anyone I know," Suzy said. James couldn't argue with that. "I appreciate you coming and all. Offering me a job."

"And you've got it."

"Pixie and I, we didn't want to tell anyone. Nothing is really going on. I mean, when he gets bored I'm sure he'll move on, and I don't want people looking at me with pity in their eyes."

"They won't."

"They will. I've seen what happened with Leo and Paul. I don't want to have to deal with that, or I will leave, for sure."

He chuckled. "Then I won't say anything. I'll mention that I know to Pixie though. I don't like lying to my brother."

"He doesn't seem to like lying either. It's always easier for him to avoid the truth."

James finished his coffee, enjoying talking to her. "I better head out. You start tomorrow, and I'll take you on a tour. Pixie will probably be there to assist."

"He likes to be hands on, doesn't he?" she said, then blushed.

"I'm not that intimately connected to my brother, Suzy. I'll take your word for it."

"You're doing it on purpose now. Making me blush."

"Just a little."

James stood up and made his way back toward the door. Stopping with his hand on the door, he turned to look at her.

"I love my brother, and yes, he's an asshole who doesn't have any filter, but with you, he's different."

"What do you mean?"

"Do you think he cares to keep a secret about the women he's screwed? He can have anyone, and often does. I clean up his messes, as he moves from woman to woman, trying to find the one that will allow him to settle. I don't know if that woman is you, but I do know that in the time frame you've given me, he hasn't been with another woman."

"Why are you telling me this?"

"So you'll be careful, and consider the fact that Pixie may have feelings for you."

"Do you really think so?" she asked.

"I know my brother, and he doesn't do this for anyone. He has feelings for you. He might not even know them yet."

"It just seems a little surreal, is all," she said.

"Don't give up on him, and don't cheat on him."

"I'm not that kind of woman."

"I don't think you are."

James left the apartment, determined to help Pixie and Suzy any way that he could. They both deserved some kind of happiness.

****

Pixie sat outside of the clubhouse on the swing, and smoked his cigarette. He was waiting for his brother to return, or for a call from Suzy to let him know something had happened.

The thought of her leaving was like a kick to the gut. It wasn't something he wanted to think about, or handle.

"What's got you sat out in the cold on your own?" Caleb asked.

"Nothing."

"Ah, I see we both are here because of nothing."

He laughed. "You're here for Kitty Cat. Me, I'm just here because I can think."

Caleb was a club brother, and a Dominant, who currently had something going down with the club's woman, Kitty Cat. She wasn't really the club woman. Kitty Cat was a woman they had found in an awful condition, and they had taken care of her. She was a submissive woman to the core, and had asked Caleb to Dominate her.

Their relationship was somewhat complicated, and it wore on the two of them daily.

"It's nothing. I'm just being a fucking pussy to be honest. I don't know. I don't get shit anymore when it comes to people, women, relationships," Caleb said.

"You're in love with Kitty Cat."

"And other than spanking her ass, and doing some random scenes, she wants nothing to do with me. I can't even help her afterward."

Pixie said nothing.

"No shitty thing to say?" Caleb asked.

"Let's just say I've got my own troubles. Women, huh."

"I wouldn't change a thing about her," Caleb said. "She is the most beautiful woman I've ever known. I love her more than anything."

Pixie took a long drag on his cigarette, wondering what was going on with James and Suzy. What job would James come up with? Would Suzy do it?

Crap. He was a fucking bundle of nerves.

"This have anything to do with Suzy?" Caleb asked.

"Nothing at all."

"You're not looking all that convincing when you say that."

His cell phone started to ring, and he smirked. "Saved for another day." He got up from the swing, and walked away from Caleb, answering Suzy's call. "Hey, baby."

"You sent James here."

"I didn't send James there. I asked him if there was a possibility of hiring you. I take it you've got a job?"

"Yeah, at the club. Everything has to be top secret, and I can't share any information or anything. There was a condition to him hiring me."

"What was it?"

"He wanted to know the truth about us."

"And what did you say?"

"I told him the truth. I need this job. The last thing I want to do is move out of Greater Falls. I like it here. I'll take whatever job I can get."

"Apart from screwing me."

"I like doing that. Do you really want me to turn that into a job?"

He chuckled. "I'll be on my way over. Chloe's not coming home until tomorrow right. With you working here, I might be able to steal you away during your break."

"Don't push it."

Pixie laughed. "What did James say?"

"Not a lot. He wants me to be careful." She chuckled. "Asked if I was pregnant."

The thought wasn't disgusting to Pixie, and he frowned. What would it be like to get Suzy pregnant? He imagined her swollen with his kid, her tits huge, and her stomach round, smiling as he came home.

Resting against the wall of the clubhouse, he took a deep breath.

Fuck, he wanted that. More than anything he wanted to come home to Suzy, and to his family.

"Pixie, you okay?"

"Yeah, yeah, I'm fine. Did he laugh?"

"No, he was pleased we used protection. It was really weird to be honest. It felt like he was more your father than your brother."

Pixie snorted. "In a way he is. He's always taken care of me, and has always been there for me when I needed him."

"You love him?"

"Sometimes more than I can even understand."

"Wow, you're being really honest."

"Babe, I'm always honest with you."

"Okay, the skirt I wore three days ago, did it make my ass look fat?"

"Totally."

"Pixie!"

"But I loved it. Your ass was begging for me to spread you open, and lick from your cunt to your little asshole. You haven't let me claim that little virginity, but I've been able to claim everything else."

She sighed. "You're not helping."

"I'm coming now. You better be completely naked for me when I get there."

Before she could say anything, he hung up.

"I've got to head out. Everything will work out with Kitty Cat."

Caleb nodded yet didn't look convinced.

"What is it?" Pixie asked.

"It's nothing. Forget it. Go and enjoy whatever it is you're going to go do."

Pixie didn't wait around. The Kitty Cat and Caleb shit was too much for him to deal with. He understood why both kept each other at arm's length, but at the same time, he figured they could help heal each other.

As he made his way to his bike, James entered the grounds. Instead of leaving, he waited for his brother.

"Thank you," he said.

"No need to thank me, Pixie. I don't mind helping Suzy. She's a good girl."

"I know."

James stared at him. "She means something to you."

"Yes."

"I'm being serious here. I'm not bullshitting with you. What are your feelings for Suzy?"

"I don't know. I can't imagine a day without seeing her." Pixie smiled. "I even went into town once just so I could see her face. Yeah, I'm turning into some kind of stalker."

"I've never seen you like this with a woman

before."

"I've never felt like this before. I don't know. She makes me happy, crazy, and she makes me want to be better for her," Pixie said. "I'm heading over to see her. Don't tell anyone about us."

"Cora will know."

"She's your woman. Ask her not to tell anyone."

James raised his brow.

"Please, I don't ask for much."

"You ask for more than enough."

"Please."

"Two pleases in one day." James reached out, touching his head, and Pixie swatted him away. "Are you okay?"

"I'm more than okay. Will you do it?"

"Yes, yes, don't worry. Your secret affair will remain so for as long as you need it."

"Thank you."

"Be careful, Pixie. I don't want you to get too involved."

"Worried I'll get hurt?"

"Yes."

"Don't worry about me. I'll take care of myself." Pixie slapped him on the shoulder then straddled his bike.

Taking off out of the clubhouse, he made his way back toward Suzy's apartment. He spent so much time there, it was starting to feel like he actually lived there.

Parking his bike up, he hummed as he travelled up the same stairs, and got to her apartment. He didn't bother knocking. Instead, he used the key he'd semi-stolen. It wasn't really stolen. Yes, he'd stolen a set of keys in order to get this key, but *it* wasn't stolen.

He closed and locked the door behind him.

The apartment was silent, and there wasn't even a

sound coming from Fluffy. His dick was rock hard, and he wanted inside her again.

Removing his leather jacket, he started getting naked as he made his way toward her room.

When he entered, he saw her lying on the bed, legs spread, and playing with her beautiful pussy just as he'd showed her. She looked fucking perfect, and he was so horny from watching her.

"Now that is a sight I could get used to."

He removed his boots and jeans. Standing naked before her, he wrapped his fingers around his cock.

This was his domain. He was king in the bedroom, and he could do whatever the hell he wanted. Suzy had given him permission, and he intended to take it.

"Give me a taste."

She stopped playing with her pretty pussy, and knelt up, offering her fingers for him to suck. Holding her wrist, he sucked her cream-drenched fingers, tasting her.

"Delicious," he said, noticing her blushing cheeks.

Sliding his fingers up the inside of her thigh, he touched her slit, finding her soaked already.

"Baby, you're so wet for me."

He thrust a finger inside her, pumping in and out before moving it against her clit, stroking her.

"Please," she said.

"You know I like to play." He took her hand, and wrapped it around his dick. Showing her exactly what he wanted, he released her hand, and focused on her pussy. Finding her clit, he pinched the nub, listening to her moan.

With each tease, the more her arousal grew until her cum soaked his hand. He loved making her so wet.

When he finally fucked her, she was always screaming and begging for more. "I'm going to have you screaming my name so loud that when you're talking to my brother tomorrow your voice is hoarse."

"Please, Pixie."

"What do you want, baby?"

"I want you. I need you. Please."

"You want me to fuck you?"

"Yes. I want it so badly."

"You want me to fuck your pussy."

"Yes."

She ran her hands up and down his dick.

Pulling his fingers from her cunt, he licked the cream right off. "Suck my dick, baby."

Chapter Three

Moving off the bed, Suzy went to her knees before him. Something happened to her when he was in control. She loved the way Pixie took charge, and there was no fighting. Neither of them battled anything when they were together in this moment. She submitted to him, and he dominated her. It wasn't a BDSM thing. He was the man, and she was the woman.

Her pussy was on fire for him, and the more he prolonged it, the more aroused she became.

Wrapping her fingers around the length of his dick, she saw the pre-cum gathering out of the little tip at the top. Flicking her tongue over it, she relished the guttural sounds he made. His whole body seemed to shake with the simple touch of her tongue.

"You have no idea what you do to me. You suck cock so damn good," he said.

She moaned around his dick, taking more of him to the back of her throat. She took him as deep as she could without retching.

"Fuck, baby." He pumped his hips, and she released his cock to hold onto his thighs. Glancing up at him, she saw he was staring down at her.

He gripped her hair and held onto her, taking over the pace she used.

Slowly, he started to fuck her face, and she sucked him in deep. When he hit the back of her throat, he didn't pull back immediately. He waited a few seconds, and finally pulled back. Bracing his legs, he started to take long, steady thrusts, moving inside her mouth as he did.

"I love seeing my dick in your mouth. It's so much better than my imagination."

He loved talking throughout, and she loved

hearing him. His voice made her forget about her fears and worries, and she focused all on him.

"Take all of it." He thrust into her mouth, and normally she would have withdrawn, but this time, she relaxed and took him as deep as he wanted to go. Staring up into his eyes, she trusted him to know what to do with her body.

Tears came to her eyes, and he pulled back, giving her time to catch her breath. He did this several times before pulling away. He dropped down to his knees, took hold of her face, and slammed his lips down on hers. She wrapped her arms around his neck, and pulled him in close. Her body pressed up against his, and she loved how hard he was to her softness. His chest, arms, and back were covered in tattoos. She loved tracing over them when they were alone.

He broke away from the kiss and trailed his lips down her neck, sucking on her pulse, flicking his tongue across down to her breasts, and over her nipples. She licked her suddenly dry lips, moaning as he captured a nipple and sucked it into his mouth. He sucked one nipple hard, then moved onto the next, sucking her into his mouth. She opened her eyes, and saw them in the mirror across from the bed. He was so much bigger than she was, in every single way.

Being with Pixie made her feel small, delicate, different.

"I need to taste you."

He stood, grabbing her and pushing her to the bed. Before she could do anything else, he had her legs spread, and was resting between them.

She went to her elbows, and watched as he swiped his tongue through her pussy. Screaming his name, she closed her eyes, loving the way his tongue danced over her clit. He slid down, fucking inside her before moving back up to suck her clit.

Pushing her pussy up to his face, she ran her fingers into his hair, holding onto his head as she did.

He flicked her clit. His movements were slow, and she loved it when he took his time. Sometimes a quickie was not what she enjoyed. There were times and places for that. On rare occasions they got her apartment and they were able to take their time. Since Grace had moved out, and Chloe began to go steady with Richard, they had more time.

Suddenly, Pixie stopped, and got off the bed, leaving her hanging.

"What are you doing?" she asked.

"It's time for me to show you my little toy."

She had looked all over the bedroom, and couldn't find it.

He moved over the bed so that his dick was in her face. Rolling her eyes, she looked up to find him pulling a small brown paper bag from beside the bed. He'd hidden it between her drawers and bed.

"You made sure I couldn't find it."

"You'd throw it out."

He sat back, and she sat up, waiting to see what he had for her.

What he pulled back had her shaking her head. "No, Pixie."

"You haven't tried it."

Her cheeks heated, and she glared at him. "It's an out hole!"

"And I'm asking you to trust me, and it will be amazing."

Tucking her hair behind her ear, she bit her lip. They had done a lot together in the past year. Pixie kept trying to take it to the next step.

She didn't know how anyone could want to have

anal sex, and that was what he wanted.

"This is a starter kit."

"Pixie?"

"Please, look, if you don't like it, we'll stop, and I won't push for it."

"Why do you want to do this?" she asked.

"I want you."

"You have me."

"No, I want to own every part of you."

"Is this some kind of weird guy thing?"

"Nope. This is just me. I want every part of you." He stroked her cheek and leaned in kissing her lips.

This was where she questioned if she knew the real Pixie. He seemed almost possessive in his need for her.

He held up a very small dildo, some lube, and she even noticed a chocolate bar.

"You're going to bribe me with chocolate?"

"Why not? It works for every other woman."

She glared at him, climbing off the bed. "You're going to mention how you've fucked every other woman!" She stormed out of her room, glancing over her shoulder to see him following her. "Asshole!"

"I've never needed chocolate to convince a woman to sleep with me, or to fuck their ass."

"Oh, and that is supposed to be a good thing. So now I'm too hard, and you need to convince me to screw with chocolate."

He growled. "You're turning everything I say around."

"Am not!" She whirled around, not caring that she was completely naked. "You're being a pain in the ass, and difficult. You're not fair."

She folded her arms, glaring at him. The mention of other women made her so angry, so upset, and it made her want to cry.

Gritting her teeth, she didn't want to think of him with other women, more experienced women. She had been a virgin, and didn't know any tricks to keep a man. The thought of Pixie with other women hurt her. She was jealous, and again that just made her so angry. It wasn't like she didn't know the kind of man he was. She knew who he was, and he was a horrible person.

With the sweetest nature he keeps hidden.

"How many women have you fucked in the ass? Why don't you go back to them, and let them have what they want? I'm too frigid for you to handle."

Tears started to fall, and she wiped them out of the way.

"Suzy," he said, his voice very soft.

"What?"

"Look at me."

Gritting her teeth once again, she focused on him. He kept his distance, and she couldn't help but take in his naked form. Pixie was a sexy, well-built, god of a man, which made everything so unfair.

It only served to make her more insecure. He was in a club surrounded by women who would do anything for him. She was afraid. No, not only afraid, but skittish as well. What if it really hurt?

"I wasn't comparing you to any woman that has been in my bed," Pixie said. "In fact, I never give other women much care. They tend to want to do things dirty with the club. They don't need chocolate."

"Why say it then?"

"Oh, because women love chocolate, and that's why I did the comparison."

"Oh," she said.

"I'd never compare you, Suzy. No other woman can ever compare to you."

"How can you say that?" she asked.

"How can I not?"

"I was a virgin. Don't you ever get bored telling me what to do?"

He laughed, and that didn't help. Spinning on her heel, she walked toward her fridge, and before she could open it, he caught her arm, and slammed her against it. It wasn't hard, and she glared at him. "What the hell are you doing?"

"I'm going to give you a bit of a reality check right now."

"Pixie."

"Shut up. I've done a lot of shit for you over the past year. I've kept us a secret, and it was you that told my brother today. Now, yes, you were a virgin, and I wasn't expecting that. I admit it freely."

She went to argue with him again, but he stopped her by pressing his palm over her face stopping her.

"I told you to shut up, and I meant it. You can talk back to me when I'm done but until then, shh!"

Suzy wanted to glare at him but relaxed, waiting for him to finish.

"You being a virgin took me back, but I like it. I know I'm an asshole when I say this, but I like the fact no one else has touched you. You're all mine, and no other man will ever know how damn hot and sexy you are. I mean it, Suzy. I haven't touched another woman since I've been with you, even before I've been with you. I got you the chocolate as a joke, and hoped we could share it. I want to do everything with you, know your whole body." Slowly, he removed his hand. "I'm speaking the truth."

"The chocolate was for us to share?"

"Yes. I didn't even think of other women."

"I believe you. I overreacted." She ran fingers

through her hair. "I'm so sorry."

"You don't have to be sorry. Just allow me to actually talk to you."

"I will. I promise."

****

Late that night Pixie stared up at the ceiling with Suzy curled up against him. He'd seen the sadness in her eyes, and also the fear. She really didn't think she was good enough for him, and that was so far from the truth.

He wanted to own every single part of her, all the time. He couldn't even recall a time when he didn't think about her, need her. James and Drake had each talked about their need, and he'd always thought it would be a nightmare. Never had he known jealousy like he did with Suzy. When he'd visited her at work, it had driven him crazy watching men flirt with her.

She never saw it, but then, she wasn't a guy.

Turning to look at her, he stroked a finger down her cheek. She sighed, and snuggled in against him. He should leave, but each day that he fell asleep with her in his arms it got harder to leave her.

After their little argument, they had eaten something, watched a little television, and then made love well into the night.

Suzy sighed and ran her hand across his chest. "Are you leaving tonight?" she asked, startling him.

"I thought you were asleep."

"I was." She held him a little tighter. "You don't have to leave if you don't want to."

"You sure?"

"You're the one who always left. I never actually told you to." She rested her head on his chest. "You're so comfortable."

He didn't want to leave.

"I'm going to stay here."

"Okay."

Wrapping his arms around her, he kissed the top of her head, and closed his eyes. Sleep came to him quickly.

There was no way he'd been asleep all that long before an alarm was blaring, and waking him up.

Opening his eyes, he glanced down to see Suzy moaning as she rolled over, and turned her alarm clock off.

Even though he didn't feel like he'd been sleeping all that long, it was still the best sleep he'd ever had.

"Crap, I've got to get ready." She climbed out of the bed, and he watched her ass wiggle as she left the room.

He could get used to this.

She appeared back in the bedroom. "Do you have anywhere else to be?"

"I'll take you to the club, but right now, I have another little problem."

"What problem?" she asked.

He moved the blanket out of the way, showing off his morning wood.

"Don't all men have that?"

"Yep."

She folded her arms. "What exactly do you want me to do with that?"

"Come here." He held his hand out, and she moved toward him. Pixie took hold of her hand, and pulled her so that she fell against him. He moved her so that she straddled his lap.

"Now, I've got something even better." He lifted her up, and aligned his cock against her entrance.

Sliding a finger inside her, he found she was already wet.

"It looks like someone else is having a little morning problem."

"I liked being in your arms all night."

He helped her lower down onto his dick. They were naked together, and he knew he should stop, and put on a condom. He didn't want to though. There was no way she was getting rid of him, and he wanted to own every part of her.

The feel of her naked pussy gripping him drove him crazy.

"You're so fucking perfect," he said.

"This is what you wanted?" she asked.

"Hell yeah, this is the way I should wake up every morning." He gripped her hips, and moved her up and down his shaft, driving deeper inside her.

Suzy moaned, and he watched his dick disappear within her body, her perfect cunt gripping him tightly as he fucked her.

"Please, Pixie," she said.

"Give it to me, baby." Releasing her hips, he slipped his fingers through her slit and started to stroke over her clit. Her teeth sank into her lip as she tried to contain her sounds. "I want to hear you scream my name. Don't fight it. Give it all to me."

"It feels so good, Pixie, so good."

"I know." He teased her clit, feeling each little quiver and tightening of her cunt around his cock. She felt fucking wonderful, and he didn't want it to stop. In fact, he wanted to fill her with his spunk, and do it all over again. Pixie waited until she came, flooding his dick with her cream, and then he flipped her onto her back, and rode her hard.

He grabbed her hands, pinning them on either side of her head, claiming her lips at the same time as he fucked her pussy. He branded her as his own. Suzy belonged to him. One day soon he hoped for the whole of the club to know the truth so he didn't have to hide it anymore.

There was no other woman for him. He'd accepted it, and now he wanted her to accept it as well.

Letting go of her hands, he glided his down to cup her hips. He didn't release her lips, kissing her throughout as his orgasm started to build. The kiss went deeper as his release rushed through him. Spilling his cum into her pussy, he filled her up. At the back of his mind, he wondered if he'd get her pregnant.

You shouldn't do this.

Pulling back from the kiss, he moved his hands to cup her face. "Hey," he said.

She smiled at him. "That is some way to wake up in a morning."

"It's good."

"Yes, it is."

A spark of guilt rushed through him.

"What's the matter?" she asked.

"Nothing. Chloe comes back today."

"Oh, yeah, she does."

"I'm thinking we need to come up with a plan so we can spend some time together."

"We find ways of being together all the time." She cupped his cheek. "We'll figure it out."

"Why don't we just tell people? My brother knows."

"I don't know. I guess I'm just a little nervous that people will treat me differently."

"Why?"

"You're known for leaving brokenhearted women with other men. Your brother, or whoever you share your women with. I don't want to deal with that."

Pixie was starting to really hate his reputation.

"I liked sleeping with you."

"I did as well." She lifted up and pressed a kiss to his lips. "I don't want to be late for work."

"Okay. Let's get dressed, and I'll treat you to breakfast at Teri's place."

"Oh, goody."

"Hey, I just made you come really well, and you're more excited about eating."

"I'm hungry."

She nibbled the back of his hand, and he laughed.

"Get dressed, and just go with jeans or something. It's an MC so nothing fancy. Last thing I need is for guys to be checking you out. Second thoughts, don't go with the jeans. I don't think I can stand to have guys checking out your ass. It's all mine to check out. Do you have jogger pants, or a white suit that makes you look insane?"

"Shut up, Pixie. I'll dress like I did for my last job. Will that be acceptable to you?"

"Not really."

"Ugh! You're just going to have to deal with it."

Pressing a kiss to her pursed lips, Pixie pulled out of her, and avoided actually looking at her pussy. He wondered what it would look like to see his own cum spilling from her lips.

Another time.

She jumped off the bed, and rushed toward the bathroom. So far there was no screaming or throwing shit, so he went to Chloe's bathroom and took a pee. Staring at his reflection in the mirror, he shook his head.

"I did what I had to do."

His reflection didn't look happy, which was crazy because he was staring at himself.

You shouldn't have done it.

Closing his eyes, he finished his business, flushed

the toilet, and washed his hands. All the time he was aware of what he'd done. Did Suzy even know or was she too distracted to care?

Leaving the bathroom, he found her back in the bedroom, finishing with the buttons on her shirt.

"Are you okay?" she asked. "You look a little troubled?"

"Nothing. Just wondering how your first day is going to go."

"You're actually a real sweetheart, you know that?"

"Totally. I'm a catch. You should consider yourself lucky." He pulled up his jeans, then left the room to find his shirt on the floor.

By the time he was dressed, Suzy was finishing with her ponytail, and they were both ready. "I'm riding my bike, so you're going to have to hold onto me."

She rolled her eyes. "Of course."

He chuckled.

"Oh, wait, I'll just leave Chloe a note for when she gets back. Let her know not to worry."

He waited as she did that, admiring her rounded ass. It wasn't long before they were on his bike, heading toward the diner.

The guilt didn't go away. It wouldn't take long, but he'd soon forget what he did, and he wouldn't care. Providing Suzy stayed with him, he was more than willing to get her pregnant. It was a last resort, but it was something he had to do.

Chapter Four

It didn't take long for Suzy to discover that James needed a secretary, a PA, a miracle, as she looked through all of his paperwork. He never filed anything, nor did he have it any kind of order.

"How do you do your taxes?" she asked.

"I have people who deal with it. They charge me a fortune to go through all the crap."

"How do they go through it?" She looked at all of the paperwork and the notes, and it was a little confusing. "This is all over the place."

"Then it's good that you need a job because I need someone to deal with this."

"Have you just employed me as your PA?"

"Pretty much."

"An MC needs a PA?"

"I own the diner as well as the main bar out front. We have some customers here every night, and I deal with everything."

"This has been happening for the past five years?"

"Seven, actually."

She shook her head, staring at the paperwork.

"Do you want the job or not? Can you even do it?"

"Don't even think of being a smart-ass. I can do this. I'll have to spend a couple of weeks going through all of this, and I'll deal with your other stuff, before I start on your present stuff."

"Good." James sat down at his desk, and proceeded to bring out multiple large boxes. "Here is everything related to the club, and here is a contract that I had Richard write up for me."

He handed her a quick sheet of paper, and she

read through it. It was an employment contract. This one demanded her being quiet about what she saw, and never letting anyone know what was going on.

"If you talk or let anyone know what you see, you're gone without pay."

"I won't say anything. I swear, I'm good at keeping a secret. Most of my friends are part of your club."

"I know, but this is more personal."

"I get it. You can trust me." She signed her name, and smiled up at him. "Thank you so much for giving me this chance."

"You should really thank Pixie. He's the one that asked."

"I'll let him know." She really did owe Pixie a lot. Even with the mountains of paperwork, she was happy.

"Right, get to work."

Staring at the boxes of paperwork, she took a deep breath, and immersed herself in her work. After twenty minutes there was a knock on the door, and James called for whoever it was to come inside.

Kitty Cat entered, and Suzy sent her a smile.

"Here you go," she said. "I've also got you a coffee, Suzy."

"Thank you."

"Got a lot of work there."

"I'm happy to do it." She took a sip of the scalding coffee before putting it on the table. She had four different piles, and that was just going by year. She was starting at the beginning and working her way back.

Throughout the day, men came to visit James. Leo and Paul entered, complaining about the women that were not looking for long term. She was surprised to hear of the two men looking for forever. They didn't seem to care that she was there, listening to it all.

Lunch came from Teri, and she walked in carrying two plates. When Suzy glanced at the clock, she saw it was a couple hours past lunch time.

"Here you go. Sorry it's late, I was experimenting. I'm surprised you haven't quit."

"I kind of like a challenge, and this is totally what this is, a complete challenge." Suzy let out a breath. "I think I'll be working here until I die."

"I hope by that time all of this is dealt with," James said. "I'm not paying you to fail."

Suzy chuckled. "I'll get it done."

"I got you a veggie burger. I'm experimenting again," Teri said, flopping down onto the sofa opposite her.

"What was wrong with your last burger?"

"Nothing. I got bored of making it, and when I get bored, I know it's time to move on and jazz it up a little. Take a bite, and let me know what you think."

Teri was one amazing cook. The best, actually, and the diner was the best in the world. She didn't just serve fast diner food. She was constantly changing the menu, and putting her own spin on everything.

Taking a bite, Suzy closed her eyes.

"Now, I didn't put mayo as a spread, but I put a spicy kind of yogurt sauce thingy," Teri said.

"That has to be the best way to eat vegetables."

"You really think so?" she asked, nibbling her lip.

"Teri, you know it's perfect," James said. "What I don't get is why I'm having to eat it. I like meat."

Teri blew a raspberry. "You know being a man doesn't have anything to do with the amount of meat you consume."

"I like meat. Beef, chicken, pork, lamb even. I'll settle for shrimp, and the occasional fish, but tofu and vegetarian is not going to satisfy me," James said, dropping the burger onto his plate.

Teri rolled her eyes, and then whistled. A second later Damon came in carrying a plate of steak and potatoes.

"That's more like it."

When Damon went to take the burger from him, James slapped his hand.

"I thought you didn't like it," Teri said.

"I still need to eat my five meals a day."

"Yeah, yeah, you're just worried that your rep is going to be ruined because you liked a veggie burger." Teri chuckled, turning toward Suzy. "I've got to head back to the diner. It's good having you around. There needs to be more women here. I need to balance things out a bit."

"Please. You know how to handle the men, and you've been doing a good job of it for a long time."

Teri smiled. "I do, don't I?" She was at the door when she turned around. "I forgot, Cora called. Ryan's in some trouble again at school, and she wanted me to tell you. She couldn't get in touch with the club."

James cursed. "I thought we'd dealt with Ryan."

"Something's not right. According to Cora, he just snapped. She saw him this morning, and he wasn't the same kid."

"I'll call Lucy. Thanks, Teri. You're the best."

"I try."

Teri left, James finished his food, and then he stood. "I've got to head out. I should be back by five, but if not, you're free to go. I'll give you a grand tour another day."

"Okay, is everything all right? Do you need my help?"

"Unless you know how to help a temperamental

teenage boy with issues, then no, this one I've got to do all on my own."

Suzy winced. "I don't. Sorry."

"Oh, well. Enjoy your afternoon, I'm going to go and see what is bothering young Ryan." Just as James was about to leave, Pixie appeared. "Excellent timing. I've got to deal with Ryan again. Will you show the lovely Suzy around? I know you don't have a problem with that."

"You got it."

"Good, good."

"Tell Ryan he needs to get his shit together."

"Before I do that, I want to know why he's decided to be an asshole."

"Should be fun. I thought boys were all assholes," Pixie said.

"No, not all of them, just some of them. Something has happened though, and I intend to get to the bottom of it."

Suzy watched as James left his office, and turned her attention to Pixie. He'd changed. The scruffy torn jeans were replaced with a fresh clean pair. "Do you like it?"

"You look good."

Quickly looking back at her work, she tried to focus on the words in front of her.

"Oh, dear, he's got you on filing."

"Yes. I need to put the last seven years into order. He must have paid a fortune for whoever dealt with his finances."

"Pretty much."

Pixie took a seat opposite her, and she was aware of him staring. It made it even harder to do her job.

"I love your hair," he said.

"The red just does it for you?"

"It's beautiful, and I love the way it fans out across my pillow, or when it's wrapped around my hand as I fuck you long and hard."

Pressing her thighs together, she stared at him. "We shouldn't be talking like this."

"I don't care what we should or shouldn't be doing. I know that I want my dick wet, and you're the only woman that can get me that way."

Her cheeks heated, but she didn't succumb. Instead, he went back to looking at the paperwork right in front of her.

"You want it, don't you? Your pussy is wet. It would love for me to spread you on this table, and show you how much I want to taste you."

"Pixie."

"Don't lie to me. You suck at it."

Staring into his eyes, she bit her lip, knowing it drove him crazy. "Maybe."

"This is going to be so much fun. I have every excuse to be here." He leaned back. "I won't interfere. Do your work, and then I'll take you on the grand tour."

****

If someone had told Pixie a year ago that he would happily sit doing nothing but staring at Suzy for hours at a time, he'd have laughed at them. He wasn't the kind of man to be controlled by a woman. He did the controlling. Suzy wasn't even begging for his attention or doing anything appealing. She was reading through paperwork, placing it in random orders.

On her lap were a pen and a notepad as she made the odd scribble here and there.

His cock thickened, and he wanted her so badly. Checking the time, he saw it was a little after five. He'd been so riveted by her that he hadn't even noticed the time.

"Time's up, and I'll let James know you worked overtime."

"Oh, crap." She stood up, and looked down at the mess. "What do I do? I've made good headway, but I don't know where to put it all."

"Leave it here, and I'll lock the office. No one will come in, and I'll talk to James when he's here."

"Awesome." She tucked behind her ears the hair that had fallen out of her ponytail. "Tour?"

"Yep." He held out his arm. "Take my arm, and I will show you the danger that is the Dirty Fuckers MC."

"You're rather playful, do you know that?"

"You inspire me."

She giggled, taking his arm. They left the office, and Pixie locked the door, pocketing the key. Just from watching her, he'd seen that she had done a lot of work today, and he didn't want her to lose any of that time.

Several of the club brothers were in the bar. Some were talking, others were doing some work, and he nodded at all of them. Each one said hello to Suzy. She was known to all of them seeing as she was friends with a couple of the club members.

"This is the main bar. We open up to some of the local couples, men and women. Most of the time we're selective. Leo and Paul will man the door for a little time, and when we have enough people, we don't allow anyone in."

"So it's not a real bar, right?"

"It is and it isn't. We don't do rowdy shit. The last thing we want is to deal with the cops being called. This is a selective club. Feel honored to be working here."

Once again, he got a giggle. He loved that sound, and intended to make her provide him with many more.

"You're a little crazy, do you know that?"

"Totally." He was crazy for her.

"You okay, Suzy?" Damon asked. He was tapping away on the computer, wearing a pair of glasses.

"You're going to ruin your cred if you keep wearing them. You're supposed to be a badass," Pixie said.

"Yeah, yeah, I'm a badass that can't see shit without them. You liking the new job?" he asked.

"It's ... interesting."

Damon chuckled. "Interesting?"

"Yeah, James doesn't understand the first meaning of order, does he?"

"Ah, he's got you on file duty. I wouldn't worry. You'll ace it."

"Thank you, Damon."

Pixie didn't like the easy banter between Damon and his woman. "Of course she'll ace it. It's why I asked James to give her a job."

"You did, did you?" Damon asked. "Pixie helping out a woman. That doesn't sound like you."

"I'm not all bad."

"You're not all good either."

"It's nothing. He's taking me on a tour, right."

"Yes, I'm taking her on a tour." Pixie gripped the back of her neck, and moved her away from the main bar.

"What the hell are you doing?"

"Why don't we tell anyone again why we're together?"

She sighed, and turned toward him. "I don't want people to pity me or change the way they see me because I'm with you."

He frowned. "You really think the club will give a shit."

"When you move on, I'm thinking things will be

different."

"What makes you think I'm going to move on?" He was trying to get her pregnant. When she'd started work for James, he'd taken a trip to the pharmacy to pick up a pregnancy when she missed her monthly cycle. She hadn't long come off her last one, so he had three weeks to get her pregnant—or he had that one time when she'd been too far gone to care.

She tilted her head to the side, and smiled. "I'm not the kind of person to believe that I'm more than enough for you." She glanced around and touched his face. "I'm happy with what I've got." She pressed a quick kiss to his lips, and withdrew. "Now, show me what has everyone in town all ready to gossip."

Pixie took hold of her hand, and another wave of guilt hit him. He was starting to get annoyed with the constant waves of guilt that were flooding him.

"Are you okay?" she asked.

"Fine, fine, don't worry about me." He took her around the various areas of the clubs, even going to the rooms where some of the club whores liked to strip for some of the locals. He let her know that he hadn't been to see any of them for a long time. He didn't need to visit anyone else when he had her.

All he needed was a pole, and some way of encouraging her to strip for him. It was a fantasy he intended to play out together soon enough.

When she'd seen everything he took her toward the back where the playrooms were. "What you're about to see, you can't tell anyone."

"This place is huge."

"It was a piece of shit when we first came here."

"Really?"

"Yeah, really. It took a long time for us to actually get everything ready for when we came to live here." He remembered the hours he'd spent stripping walls, watching electricians and plumbers working to get the house up to date. It was during that time that he'd hated the thought of settling down. Now, he wouldn't change it for the world.

"I won't say anything."

"Come on," he said, opening the door. He wasn't surprised to find Kitty Cat and Caleb in the room. Neither of them was doing much. They hadn't started a scene yet. Pixie had watched them enough times to know that this was the tension before the storm.

"Is she supposed to be here?" Caleb said.

"I'm allowed to give her the tour, and we won't disturb you. Promise."

Caleb glared but didn't say anything. Taking a seat in a booth, Pixie placed his arm across Suzy's shoulder, and sat back, watching.

The booths were dark, and Caleb moved up to Kitty Cat, and placed his hand on her back. It was rare for him to actually touch her. Pixie tensed up but was surprised to see the smile on Kitty's face.

"You want to do this?" he asked.

"Yes, Sir." She frowned.

Pixie knew why she was frowning. Rarely had Caleb approached her like this. He was breaking their ritual.

Caleb nodded. "Show me how much of a good girl you are."

Without any hesitation, Kitty went to her knees and bowed her head, offering the perfect submission.

Something seemed to come over Caleb as he growled, and walked away.

"What's going on?"

"I don't know."

Caleb paced up and down, and then moved to

stand in front of Kitty once more. Pixie tensed up as he saw a tear spill onto her leg, but what surprised him was Caleb.

"Red, fuck, red, I can't do this."

Caleb didn't wait around, and seconds later, the sound of a door slamming closed echoed around the room.

"Um, usually something happens," Pixie said.

"Kitty," Suzy said, getting up from her seat.

He went with her, helping Kitty to her feet, noticing how pale she was.

"It's fine. I'm fine." She held her hand up, smiled. "I'm sorry we didn't give you much of a show."

"I don't even know what the hell I'm supposed to be looking for," Suzy said. "Would you like to head home? You can come and hang out at my place."

Pixie didn't like that. He wouldn't be able to visit her if someone else was there. The women seemed to band together in one room.

He was turning into a sucker for this woman.

"No, no, I'm just going to stay here. I'm going to head to my room. I've got a headache."

Before either of them could say anything, Kitty Cat was gone, heading toward the backrooms.

"Is she going to be okay?"

"I hope so."

"I don't get it. What did I miss?"

"What you saw was Caleb calling their Dom/sub relationship over."

"Over?"

"Finished. I've never seen him do that before, but it has clearly got to him."

"I'm worried about her."

"Don't be. The club will keep an eye on her."

She smiled, and he rested his hands on her

shoulders. "Will you take me home?"

"Yeah, I will."

Chapter Five

When James got to the school, he was tense. He'd thought he was done with dealing with Ryan's shit. Over a year ago, Ryan had been acting out and fighting in school. Lucy, Ryan's mother was the old lady of Dane, a club brother who just got up, and left. They had tried to find him, but Dane was the kind of guy who wouldn't be found if he didn't want to. In protest, Ryan had been getting into fights, getting bad reports from the teachers. Once James had a talk with him, and let him know he or the club wasn't going anywhere, Ryan had gotten his shit together.

Entering the school, he didn't need directions, and there Cora stood, waiting for him.

"What's going on?"

"I don't know. I saw him today before school, and he told me to fuck off. Next I know, there's a fight broken out, but Ryan walked away, and then around lunchtime, he just went completely insane."

"Has Lucy turned up?"

"Yeah, and someone else."

He turned toward Cora. "Someone else?"

"Um, I think it's Dane."

"That's not possible."

She shrugged. "Lucy's in there with Sharon, and there's this big guy. Lots of ink, lots of hair as well. Looks a little unkempt."

James didn't want to believe it, but there was no other explanation for it.

"What do you want to do?" she asked.

"I want to go and see who the fuck that is."

James didn't wait for an invitation. Walking right in, he stopped when he caught sight of the three people sitting around Sharon's desk. The moment he saw him,

James knew it was Dane.

Without thinking, James launched at him, slamming his fist into the guy's face.

Women screamed, and in the distance he heard Sharon yelling for security.

"It's me, man, it's Dane."

"I know who the fuck you are. You think you can come here after all this time, and just what, do whatever the fuck you want?"

"I—"

James slammed his fist against his face, not wanting to hear another word from him.

Cora grabbed his arm and yanked with all of her might. James knew it was his woman, and he stopped immediately.

"Don't call the cops," Dane said.

"Fighting like this in front of Ryan—"

"I don't care. It's what he deserves."

James turned to Ryan. "I take it this was why you were so pissed?"

"Yeah, I shouldn't have let my temper get the better of me."

"You're right. You shouldn't. You're a better man than that, and I expect better."

Ryan nodded.

"Do we need to take him out of school?" James asked.

"He's my son," Dane said.

"Last time I checked you ran from that title. You don't get a say."

"I'm still Lucy's husband!"

"Only because they couldn't find your body, and she wasn't willing to divorce you. I'll give her a dead body if she'd like."

"James, it's okay," Lucy said. "Can I take Ryan

home?"

"Yes. I'm going to ask that he take the rest of the week to calm down, and come back to us next Monday. I don't want any more incidents like this, do you understand?" Sharon asked.

"Yes," all three said in unison.

James glared at Dane.

Turning toward Cora, he gave her a quick hug. "I'll pick you up from work."

"Okay."

On the way outside, James followed Lucy toward her car. Once she was there, she turned. "I don't want him to come with me," she said.

"Lucy—"

"He's caused too much pain, and right now, I want to deal with my son without dealing with him."

"Fine. He's coming with me to the clubhouse."

"I'm supposed to be helping my kids, my family."

"You had your chance, and what did you do? Run away." James shook his head. Pulling out his cell phone, he dialed Pixie's number. He needed his brother to come and pick him up. When no answer came from Pixie, he called Caleb. Shit was about to hit the fan in a big way.

****

Chloe was back, and because of that, Pixie couldn't linger.

"Why are you here?" Chloe asked.

"He dropped me off. I'm working at the clubhouse, and he was kind enough to bring me home." Suzy smiled at him.

One day, he was going to get her to admit that they were together. Chloe stared at him, and he shrugged. "I'm a nice guy."

She chuckled. "You're a guy who wants

something, and I know you want our little redhead."

"How was your time away with Richard?"

"It was good. We're working through our difficulties."

"Having sex?"

"Pixie!" Suzy said, glaring at him.

"No. We're not having sex. We're actually talking, a lot. I like that."

He saw the wistfulness on Chloe's face, and knew what she meant. The sex with Suzy was out of this world, but he loved it when they talked. Those few blissful moments of sharing made the secrecy all worth it.

The telephone started to ring, and Suzy was closest, picking it up.

"Hello … yeah, he's here, do you want … oh, yeah, of course." She hung up, looking toward him. "That was James. He said it was an emergency, and that Dane was back."

Pixie tensed up. "You're certain."

"Yeah, he left you messages, that's what he said, and he wants you to get back in touch, or at least get to the club."

"I'm going to have to go." He pulled his cell phone out of his pocket seeing several missed calls and texts. Fuck, he'd had it on silent, and he hadn't given it a thought. "I've got to go."

He looked toward Suzy, about to go and give her a kiss. She gave a small head shake, and he sighed. "I'll see you two lovely ladies soon. Have fun."

"You too," Chloe said.

Suzy remained silent, and it hurt a little to know she wasn't desperate to talk about their relationship.

Leaving the apartment, he headed downstairs to where he'd left his car. He'd have taken his bike but Suzy begged for him to take the car, and he just couldn't deny her.

He made his way straight to the club, and when he climbed off his bike, he saw Kitty sitting on the wall. She had a jacket wrapped around her, and he saw that she was crying.

Climbing out of his car, he went straight to her. "Are you okay, babe?" he asked.

She looked up at him. "Of course." She wiped the tears away. "Have you heard?"

"I didn't want to believe it. Dane's back."

"Yeah, and James is pissed. Ryan went off the deep end."

Pixie sighed. "Do I want to go in there?"

"It's up to you. I think it's easier to stay out here rather than go in there. He's been there for a few hours."

"Shit, I was with Suzy."

"Is something going on between the two of you?"

"What do you mean?" he asked.

"Don't play dumb, Pixie. I've known you too long."

"I'll tell you my problem if you tell me yours."

"Nothing is wrong with me."

"What about Caleb and you? You can't tell me that all is fine. I know differently." He leaned against the wall, watching her.

"I don't know what is going on between the two of us. He wants something, and I can't give him that."

Pixie laughed. "You two have always been skirting around each other. Do you think your and his relationship doesn't fuck with his head? There's a good few years between the two of you, not to mention the past. He knows what you went through, and yet he fights that every single time, and gives you what you want."

The tears were falling once again. "I know. I'm a horrible person."

"I didn't say you were horrible."

She sniffled. "I'm sorry."

He wrapped his arms around her, pulling her into a hug. "Don't worry. You've got nothing to be sorry about, but you really need to talk to him."

She nodded, and he stepped away.

"What about you and Suzy?" she asked.

He turned toward her, and smiled. "I want her all to myself all the time, and she won't give me that."

Kitty's eyes went wide. "You and Suzy?"

"Don't tell her, or you'll ruin whatever chance I've got to keep her for myself."

"My lips are completely sealed. Do you love her?" Kitty asked.

Pixie stared at her. "I'm going to head inside." He wasn't ready to admit his feelings yet. Suzy was an enigma to him most of the time, and he didn't want to risk the rejection.

You sound like a pussy. You want to get her pregnant, but you won't admit to wanting her.

He made his way inside the clubhouse, and noticed that all of the brothers were there. The main bar wasn't open either. He noticed that when he drove around back toward the main clubhouse.

"I'm here," he said, drawing everyone's attention. Pixie didn't care, and a small path was made.

He saw Dane. The man who had just gotten up one day without a word and left.

Folding his arms, Pixie smirked. Dane had a black eye and blood spilling from his nose.

"Hello, stranger. Did you all know we've got a stranger in the house?"

Several of the brothers laughed. James didn't look happy. He was pacing the length of the club. "Where were you?"

"Taking Suzy home, and then spending a little time with Chloe, why?" Pixie asked.

"Lucy doesn't want him going home."

"It's my fucking house!" Dane growled the words out.

"Oh, it's *your* house?" Caleb asked. "Last time I checked we're the ones that have been dealing with the upkeep, and also taking care of your kids. You weren't around at all."

All of the brothers had gone to Lucy to help her. She hadn't wanted the help, but they had gone anyway. She was touched that they still considered her part of the club.

"You going to tell us what the fuck the problem was?" he asked.

Dane gritted his teeth. "I just needed some space."

"That it? That's all you're going to say?"

"Do you even know what the fuck I was dealing with?" Dane asked. "I've been married nearly twenty years. I have three kids, and apart from the club, I've done nothing. I woke up one day, and I watched everything that was going on around me, and you know what? I didn't like it. I was a father, a husband, a club member, but I was no longer Dane, the man."

"This is about your dick?" Leo asked. "You've got issues because you were only with one fucking lady?"

"I got married young, and had kids, and I just wanted it all to stop."

They all stared at Dane, and even Pixie was angry at him. If he remembered rightly, Lucy hadn't wanted to marry a fighter. The one thing they all had in common was the fact they'd once fought for Ned Walker, the king of fighters in Vegas. Dane was one of those fighters, and it was during his time that he'd found Lucy. They started the club not long after they started going steady.

James looked sickened. "I don't even want to deal with you."

"What would you have done?" Dane asked. "None of you know what it's like to be me."

"I'll beg to differ," James said. "You don't see Drake here, do you? That's because he's married with a kid. I'm also with a woman now as well. None of us back away from our responsibility. You have, and you're nothing like us. None of us would turn our backs."

The thought of walking away from Suzy and his kid made Pixie sick to his stomach. He couldn't do it, and looking at Dane, he couldn't understand it either. Lucy was a good woman. She never put any pressure on Dane. He could pretty much come and go as he pleased.

"Come on, Pixie, you know what I mean."

"I don't. You picked Lucy. You married her, and had kids. You shouldn't have left."

"What happens now?" Dane asked.

James looked around at the club. "We have to talk about this, but I'm going to go and see Lucy. You're not allowed to leave the club unless it's to leave town."

"I'm not leaving."

"Where did you go?" Pixie asked.

"Everywhere. I went to see everything."

Once, Pixie would have been lured by the need to travel. Right now, he didn't see the attraction. The only way he'd leave would be if Suzy went with him.

"It's late, James," Cora said. "Let Lucy have tonight with the kids. We'll go tomorrow."

James nodded. "Who wants security duty?"

"I'll take it," Pixie said. "I've got nothing better to do."

He wanted to be with Suzy, and if he couldn't do

that, he may as well go and help his club.

Chapter Six

"What's going on with you and Pixie?" Chloe asked.

"Nothing, why?"

They sat on the sofa eating spaghetti carbonara that Suzy had made.

"Please, I'm not an idiot, nor am I blind. Something is going on with you and Pixie."

What happened to their secrecy? For nearly a year they had been seeing each other, and no one knew about it.

"You can tell me."

"I don't know what you expect me to say."

"The truth. Are you or are you not a thing with Pixie?"

"Let's talk about yours and Richard's time away."

"We'll get to that. Come on, Suzy. I thought we were friends."

"We are friends."

"Friends share everything together."

Twirling some spaghetti onto her fork, she took a bite, and turned to Chloe. "I slept with him." Suzy didn't know what she expected to feel, but relief wasn't it. "Wow, I can't believe I said that."

"You slept together? Like recently?"

"No, not recently. It was a long time ago. Um, just under a year, I think." She shoved some more food into her mouth to stop herself from speaking.

"Oh, my God, you lost your virgin card, and you didn't tell us."

"I lost it with Pixie."

"So, who the hell cares? Did he make it good? I mean, that is almost a year, and you're still fucking him.

That has to be some kind of record for him."

Suzy winced. "Thanks."

"No, I'm serious. Pixie hasn't been sleeping with anyone."

"How do you know?"

"It's me. I know everything. I kid you not, he's not with anyone else, just you."

"How is that possible?" Suzy asked.

"Maybe he likes the whole blank canvas thing, or maybe he likes you, Suzy."

"He could have any woman he wants."

"You made him work for it."

"Not very hard," Suzy said, snorting at the idea.

"I don't know. You'd known him nearly two years, and then you finally gave in. In Pixie-timeline that's like, a hundred."

"You can't be serious."

"I'm totally serious. He's never had to work for a woman. Never ever. You're the first woman I know that he's actually stayed serious about. He hasn't been with anyone else. He could have feelings for you."

Suzy paused. She didn't even want to hope of that. When she first saw Pixie, he'd made her nervous. Like really nervous. She saw right through his act, and knew he was a player, using women and tossing them aside when he was done. She never wanted to fall victim to that. Then through Cora, Grace, and Pixie's random visits to the shop, she'd started to like him, and his attention. When they slept together, those feelings didn't change. If anything, she tried to keep him at arm's length so she didn't fall so easily.

"What's wrong?" Chloe asked.

"I don't know. I like him as well. I mean, he's not this asshole when he's with me. He makes me laugh."

"Why haven't you told anyone about you two

being together?" Chloe asked. "Are you ashamed of him?"

"No, not at all. I mean, I think I was ashamed of myself for falling for him. Just being another woman in a random bunch of women. I'm not immune to his charm." Suzy tucked some of her hair behind her ear. "The thing is, he's not the guy he makes out he is at the club. When we're alone, he's different. He's kind, and he's thoughtful, and I can't imagine being with anyone else." She stopped eating, and put her plate on the table.

"What is it?" she asked.

"When I was ill, and you and Grace weren't around, he'd bring me soup, and sit with me until you guys got home. He sat and watched reruns of some comedy show on television. The other day, he stayed all night, and I slept in his arms." She rubbed her eyes. "God, he even got me a job."

"What?"

"He's the one that got me this job with James and the club. I told him I may have to leave Greater Falls to go somewhere else. I didn't go. I'm right here because I'm going to get paid well. All James asked was for me to keep your guys' secrets, and that is exactly what I'm going to do."

"Dirty Fuckers need privacy. I'll never tell their secrets, and I don't even ask Richard about them either. I love them like a family."

Suzy stood and grabbed her plate, heading toward the kitchen. "I don't know what to do."

"What do you mean?" Chloe asked, following her.

"If I fall for him, and he picks someone else, I'm screwed. I never even thought of this when I decided to take this damn job. Ugh, I'm so stupid. How can I allow myself to be with him? I'm not the kind of woman who'll be able to stand to see him with other women!" She opened the fridge and grabbed out an orange juice.

"What if he's not like that?"

"What do you mean? It's Pixie. You've known him longer than I have. Does he strike you as the kind of guy to settle down?"

"He didn't strike me as the kind of guy to stay hunting for a girl who didn't want him."

"What does that mean?"

"It means that when it comes to Pixie, I really don't know what to expect." Chloe took a bottle of juice out of the fridge, and they both made their way back to the sofa. Collapsing down onto the plush fabric, Suzy rested her head back against it. "Do you have feelings for him?" Chloe asked.

"Yeah, I do. More than I even want to admit to. I'm a sucker. Just tell me now."

"You're a sucker, but you really can't help it," Chloe said, patting her hand. "You're good for Pixie."

"I was worried that you would all get angry with me."

"What for?"

"Giving in to Pixie."

"Sweetie, I'm not one to judge. Look at me, I spent the entire weekend with Richard, and I only got back this morning."

"How did it go?"

"It was ... different."

"Different, that sounds a little vague."

"I don't know what to make of it to be honest," Chloe said. "I wonder if the only reason we could have worked was because of the club."

"I don't get you."

"He's a Dominant. You've had the grand tour, right?"

"Yes." She hadn't seen it in action, but she didn't need to. It was all over the internet now, and in almost every single book. Grace had a thing for erotica, and stealing her e-reader, Suzy had read it. Some of them were really hot.

"Richard's a Dominant, and I'm a submissive. When we played in the club, we had our roles to play, and neither of us differed from it. Now, we're different, and it's strange."

"Good strange, or bad strange?"

"I really don't know anymore." Chloe smiled. "You ever feel like you're out of your own body, and looking in?"

"Sometimes."

"When I'm with Richard, I don't know what to expect, or if I'm playing it right."

"You shouldn't be thinking like that, Chloe. It should be natural to you."

Chloe sighed. "It sucks. It really does suck."

"Do you love him?"

"More than anything. I don't even want to think of life without him." Tears spilled down her cheeks. "I don't know. I expected something different than what is actually happening."

"Look at the two of us. Crying and moaning over men who actually want to be with us."

"Never thought it would happen," Chloe said.

"Let's watch a movie, and pretend we're normal."

Suzy settled down into the sofa as Chloe picked a movie. All of their problems would be there tomorrow.

Rubbing at her temples, Suzy forced a smile at her friend. In the back of her mind, she wished for Pixie's arms wrapped around her.

One day at a time. That was what she had to do. One day at a time.

****

"I thought if anyone was going to understand me, it would be you," Dane said.

Pixie looked up at the man that he was babysitting. "Why the hell would I understand what the hell you were doing?"

"You're like me. You need to roam free."

Pixie shook his head. "I'm nothing like you."

"You've never settled down in all the years I've known you."

"The right woman hadn't come my way, and besides, you've been gone a long time. Things change."

"Oh, so you're seeing someone?"

"Yeah, I am, actually, and it's serious."

"How serious?"

"Serious enough for me to try to get her pregnant." The words slipped out, and he cursed himself. "Just shut the fuck up. No matter what you think, this isn't going to go away. Lucy had a right to know what happened to you. You've got three kids. One of them lost his shit when you were gone, and it was up to us to pick up the pieces."

"And I appreciate that."

"You don't appreciate shit."

Pixie lifted up his cell phone and looked through the photographs he'd taken of Suzy. There were some of her with Cora, with the club, with Grace and Chloe, then a rare few of the two of them together.

"I never intended to be gone for long."

"Regardless, you were still gone. Your son felt that loss. The fucking club felt your loss." Pixie forced himself to look at Dane. "Where were you?"

"I was dealing with myself."

"You were out partying and screwing around, weren't you?"

Holy shit!

He loved her. That was what he felt for Suzy. It wasn't anything else but love. Pixie stood up, and left the room, slamming the door closed, and leaning against it before dropping down onto his butt.

He was in love with Suzy. The thought of it, the words, besides shocking him, were the utter truth. Licking his lips, he ran a hand over his face. His heart was pounding. Was this what James felt for Cora? Drake for Grace. Holy hell. Yeah, he was in the zone of being shocked right now.

Grabbing his cell phone, he dialed Suzie's number, and waited.

"Hello," she said, sounding a little breathless.

"Hey, baby," he said, smiling.

"Pixie, how are you?"

He imagined her sitting on the edge of her bed, listening to him.

"I'm good. Missing you, and wishing I was with you."

"I do as well."

"What are you doing?"

"We're watching another movie, and I'm just getting changed into pajamas. I thought you might come here, and we could have some time together."

"Wish I could, baby, but I've got to babysit. I'll be with you tomorrow, though."

"I look forward to it."

Silence fell between them, and he rubbed at his eyes. "Suzy, babe, have you been with anyone else since we've been together?"

"No, why? Have you?"

"No. I told you, this is you and me."

"Have you ever been faithful to a woman?"

"I've never committed to a woman. You're the

first in everything."

She giggled. "We're both virgins in different areas."

"We are. You'll be here tomorrow, right?"

"Of course. I've got work to do."

"Suzy, come on!"

He heard Chloe yell, and decided to let Suzy go. "I'll chat with you soon."

"Bye, Pixie."

She hung up the phone.

"I love you, Suzy." Even though she didn't hear, it felt good for him to tell her. He was pleased to actually say it.

****

Kitty walked toward Caleb's bedroom. He lived on the fourth floor, and she hadn't been here at all. Apart from being together in the playrooms, she never ventured near him out of the realms of the Dom/sub relationship.

Her heart was racing, and she rubbed her hands together, hating how nervous she felt. This man had given her heaven without crossing the line with her. Sex between them had been ... weird.

No, it hadn't been weird, it'd been perfect, and she had freaked out, keeping him at arm's length, begging him not to tell anyone.

Locking her fingers together, she counted to ten, and then before she could chicken out, she knocked on his door.

There.

No backing down.

She was petrified.

Seconds passed, and when she didn't think he'd answer, she turned to leave. The door opened.

"Kitty?"

"Hey," she said, forcing a smile to her lips.

"Crazy life, huh? Dane back and all." She ran fingers through her hair, and stared at him. "So, yeah, Lucy must be freaking or something about her husband being here." She was rambling, so she sucked her lips in and smiled. "Anyway, I don't know why I'm here, and so I'm just going to go."

Caleb reached out, stopping her. The moment he touched her, she gasped. "What's going on?"

This was the first time he'd touched her out of their life. She stared at his large hand on her arm before turning toward him.

"You're touching me," she said.

He gritted his teeth.

"I've seen you completely naked, Kitty. I've been inside you, not that anyone would know. I've spanked your ass until it was red raw, and you couldn't sit on it for a week. Denied you orgasms, and I know everything about you."

Tears filled her eyes. "I wanted to make sure you're okay. You walked away earlier, and I was worried."

"You were worried about me?"

"It's the first time you've just walked away."

"And you don't have a clue why I did that?" The anger in his voice was clear to hear.

She looked down at her clenched hands and took a deep breath. "No."

He snorted. "Of course you wouldn't. Why the hell would you think I couldn't do it this time?"

"Do what?"

"Do this with you. You ask me to spank your ass, and then not to touch you. I have to watch you crying, and I can't give you comfort."

"You don't need to."

"Yes, I do. I'm the one that caused those tears. I

should be the one to help ease those tears, but you take it away from me. You take so much away from me."

"You don't need it."

"Yes, I do!" He yelled the words, and paused, taking a deep breath. "You want to continue with our relationship in the playroom, something has to change."

"Why?"

"Because I don't want to be this kind of man. You're not giving me a chance to be a nice guy, and I am, Kitty. I would be so good for you if you gave me a chance."

"Caleb?"

"No. You want me again, you give me everything. Until then, we've got nothing to talk about."

He closed the door, leaving her alone, and knowing something had to change.

Chapter Seven

James dropped Cora off at the school, and made his way toward Lucy's home. It had been a hard night, knowing that Dane was back. Not only was Dane back but it had fucked with Ryan's head. James wasn't used to dealing with this kind of drama. The club didn't have any drama because they stayed well clear of it. This was why he'd come to Greater Falls. After a young life of fighting, and being part of Ned Walker's crew, he was done with everything else.

They didn't do drugs, nor did they deal in guns. They were one hundred percent legit. They owned the diner, and the biggest risk they took was with the stock markets. They had investments all over the place, and intended to put as much faith in Greater Falls as their future.

The club meant everything to him. Cora was the love of his life. They didn't need to get married for that love to actually mean something to him. His life, it was perfect, and now Dane was back, and he didn't trust him.

Parking his car outside of Lucy's home, James climbed out as Ryan opened the door. The boy/man before him looked sheepish, and scared.

"I'm sorry, James. I know you asked for me to be better, and I should have been better."

James held his hand up. "No need to forgive. Your father turning up, that was a big deal, and I can see that."

Ryan let out a breath. "I just, I don't know. He told us he couldn't deal, and he was sorry, but he was back now." Tears filled Ryan's eyes, and he looked away. "I just snapped."

"Everyone snaps from time to time. Being a good man, a better man, it's about being able to control that emotion."

"I know, and I completely screwed up, didn't I?"

"You screwed up your chance. When you go back to school next week, you've got no choice but to keep your head down, and to do whatever shit you need to do to graduate."

"I will."

A car pulling in on the driveway made James turn. There was Lucy. She looked pale and sad.

"Are you okay?" he asked, going to help her with the car.

"Yeah, I'm okay. Just a little tired."

"How is Lewis doing?" In the past year Lucy had grown close to a rancher, Lewis Corn. The club had him checked out, and when he'd come back clean, they were more than happy for her. None of them had expected her to constantly wait for Dane. That wasn't fair on her. Lucy was a beautiful woman who deserved a chance to find someone.

"I don't know. I called him last night. Let him know that Dane was back. It seemed wrong, deceitful to, you know, let him find out from someone else."

"I understand."

"Has he left again?" Lucy asked.

He saw the hope in her eyes, and it made James mad as hell. Dane had run from his responsibilities, and that pissed him off. "No. He's back at the club."

"Oh."

"We don't need him, Mom."

"Ryan, sweetie, go to your room, and study. I really appreciate everything you've done, but you should be in school. Please, do this for me."

Ryan looked ready to argue, and James gave him a look. Maybe there was hope for him yet. James had the look down. Now all he needed to do was knock Cora up.

He was torn in two about finally having a baby. He wanted a baby, and Cora said she'd like to have his kid one day, start a family. The biggest problem for him was he didn't want to share Cora. With a child he'd have no choice but to share her. The very thought of doing that filled him with regret. She belonged to him, so he decided against actually having a baby.

When they were alone, Lucy finally relaxed and showed him the turmoil she was in.

"I'm really glad you came."

"The club is with you."

"I truly thought you'd be with Dane."

They both made their way into the kitchen. "When you came onto the scene, we all warned him. He decided to do whatever the hell he wanted to do. You're a good woman. You didn't deserve for him to walk away."

Tears filled Lucy's eyes. "I'm glad he's back, and yet at the same time, I'm so angry. He left, and I had to struggle to find a job. He didn't give me any warning, just woke up, and left me."

"What do you want to do?"

Her hands locked together, and he saw the pain within her.

"Lucy, you don't have to hide from me. I'm not going to judge you."

"Every time I think of him, and of the situation, I just want a divorce. He's here now, and he's not dead, which means I can move on with my life."

James nodded.

"Stay here."

She left the kitchen, and he finished making them a drink. Seconds later she came in holding the divorce paperwork.

"Could you give this to him, and ask him to sign

it?"

"If he doesn't?"

"Tell him if he ever loved me at all, even just a little, then to just sign the forms." She held out the divorce papers. "I'm in love with Lewis, James. It was hard for me to move on, but we haven't gone further in our relationship."

Her cheeks flushed, and she looked away.

"You haven't had sex with him?"

"No, I haven't."

"Wow, and you love him. That's pretty deep."

"I hope it doesn't upset you."

"Lucy, you'll always be dear to the club. All you have to do is call, and we'll come running to you." He held his arms open, and she went into them.

"Thank you, James. For everything."

"You've got nothing to thank me for."

****

Grace and Drake came back early with Joseph, and they entered the club, and of course chaos ensued. All it took was one look at Dane, and Drake was shouting. Pixie didn't get involved. Instead, he'd gone into town, collected Suzy from her apartment, and left her in James's office. He was looking at a potential vacation away from Greater Falls, and all the crap happening in the club.

Dane was a problem.

Caleb and Kitty were having problems.

Ryan was a problem.

Richard was moody as fuck. He'd come into the club late last night to drink.

Pixie didn't want to deal with any of this shit, so he held a catalogue promising fun, sunshine, and lots of hot sex.

"Where you heading?" Kitty asked.

"Away from all this crap." He didn't look up from the catalogue.

"I'm sure Suzy would love a trip away."

"How do you even know it's her?" He looked up at her.

"Quite easy. She's the only one you've been interested in, and the women talk. You, my friend, haven't been sleeping with anyone for a long time. The only person you've been seen with is Suzy."

He rolled his eyes. "Women irritate me."

"Thank you," she said, smiling.

"What's going on with you and Caleb?"

He saw her gaze darken, turning toward Caleb.

"Nothing."

"You know that man loves you more than anything, right?" Pixie asked. He never meddled. Fuck, he never got involved in anything like this, and yet, this was exactly what he was doing. It baffled him.

"He deserves someone better than me."

"Better than you."

"Yeah, better than me, Pixie. He deserves a woman that can accept his touch without waiting for the pain." She took a deep breath. "Let's move on to you and Suzy. It's much more fun planning someone else's future than thinking of my own." She leaned over, staring at the picture before her. "Beautiful," she said. "Suzy would love that."

"You think?"

"Yeah. When are you taking her?"

"I don't know." He got to his feet. "I will go and see."

Leaving Kitty alone, he made his way into James's office. She looked up, smiling. "Hey."

"Hey. So I've been thinking."

"All right," she said, placing her paperwork back

91

on the table. She turned toward him. "I'm listening."

"We need to spend some time alone. Away from the chaos of the club, and the people we're close to." He sat on the sofa and opened the booklet. "I want to book us a two-week vacation here."

Pixie wanted her all to himself where he could enjoy being with her.

"It's a Caribbean island. I can't afford—"

"I can."

"Pixie?"

"No, I want us to go away together. Would you go with me?"

"In a heartbeat."

"Then we'll go."

"I just started a new job, and I don't want to push James—"

"Already on it. You'll go with me if I can get you time away?"

"Yes. I'd love to go with you."

Pixie leaned over, pressing a kiss to her lips. "You're amazing." He so wanted to tell her he loved her. Instead, he kept those words to himself, and simply focused on making her smile.

"No, you're amazing, Pixie." She wrapped her arms around him, pressing her body against him.

Dropping the booklet, he held her close, pressing kisses to her neck, wishing they were alone. "Last night was torture."

"Chloe knows."

"A lot of people know about us," he said. "Does that bother you?"

"Right now, not so much." She moaned.

They were interrupted by shouting coming from the other room. Pixie groaned. "And so the chaos begins."

She giggled. "Is it wrong I just want you to close the door, and take care of me?"

"Are you feeling horny?"

"Yeah, I think I am."

"From virgin to horny. Damn, I'm good." He pressed a kiss to her, and got up. "Be ready for this weekend."

"That soon?"

"I'm an awesome person. I'll get this done." He pressed another kiss to her lips, and left the room.

"This is horseshit," Dane said, staring at several official papers. "She wants a divorce?"

"Yes, she wants a divorce. She wants nothing from you, nothing at all," James said.

Pixie watched as Dane stared at the paperwork, and shook his head. "No, I didn't agree to this. I came back for her."

"You left her," James said. "You cheated on her. There's a man she wants to be with, and she hasn't because of you. You owe her this."

"I want to talk to her."

James took a deep breath. "She wants nothing to do with you. Just sign the paperwork."

"I love her."

Pixie watched as his brother flung his head back, and laughed. "You love her? Your ass hasn't even been in Greater Falls when she needed you most. She asked me for one thing, and I'm going to make sure she gets it."

James turned away and made his way toward his office. Suddenly, he stopped and made his way toward the kitchen. Pixie rushed for him.

"Hey, James, I want to take Suzy on a romantic vacation, and she would be willing to go with me but she's working for you, and so I figured if you'd be a star brother, and let her go with me, you never know, the trip could give you a niece and nephew, one or the other, or both."

James stopped holding his hand up. "Whoa. You are talking way too fast for me right now."

"Oops, sorry." He pretended to lock his lips and throw away the key.

"Are you five now?"

"I love her," he said, spilling the words he felt.

James paused.

"Yeah. You heard me right. I love her, and I want to spend the rest of my life with Suzy." So much so he'd gone and pierced every single one of his condoms with a damn needle. The guilt was gnawing away at him. He was used to getting what he wanted, and he wanted Suzy all to himself.

James stared at him. "What's her favorite color?"

"Pink. She tries to pretend it's not, but it really is."

"What about the food she likes?"

"She likes hot and spicy food. Trying new things, and she does enjoy cooking even if some of the stuff she cooks really doesn't work out. Why are you asking me these questions?"

"It's the first time you've ever cared enough to find out about a woman. Usually, you're all about what you want, what you need."

"Did I pass some kind of test?" Pixie asked.

"Yeah. Suzy can go on vacation. I've got stuff to deal with, and the mountain of paperwork will still be here when you both get back."

"Do you need me for club stuff?"

"No. I can handle everything."

Pixie nodded. "She's the real deal, James."

"I'm happy for you. I wish I can tell you how

much, but right now, I just have to deal with Dane right now."

"So, Lucy wants a divorce?"

"Yes. She wants a chance with Lewis."

"I don't blame her."

"Dane cheated on her. You know that."

"I figured as much. The guy was never a monk. Lucy deserves some peace after the crap he's put her through."

"I couldn't agree more with you," James said. "When will you be leaving?"

"I'm hoping for tonight. I've got to rush through the arrangements."

"I'll call if I need anything."

"You're a good man, James. No one can question that."

James nodded. "Thank you."

"Only speaking the truth." Pixie smiled at him. "You're doing the right thing."

"Go and order your vacation. I'm going to handle this mess."

****

Chloe grabbed the latest plate full of food. The diner was busy today, and her feet were hurting her even in the flats. Teri hadn't been able to come out, and neither of them had greeted Grace and Drake with their son Joseph.

"Let me help," Grace said.

"No, you're not due back for a couple of days. We can handle this rush. I'll be back to take your order in a second," Chloe said, passing their table. Putting the two plates down on the table, she smiled. "Is there anything else I can get you?"

The two men were local, and occasionally visited the club.

Dane didn't say a word, and Pixie forced a laugh. "This is what it's about? You think you didn't get enough pussy before the club?"

"I was married."

"When we fought for Ned Walker, Dane, there were enough groupies for you to have more than your fair share. If I recall, you did. You had your fair share, and then some before Lucy came. Once she was there, no other woman would do. You wanted *her*. We warned you about settling down. You said you were ready, and I have to say, you convinced me. Now you're saying that you weren't."

Silence fell between them.

"I just, I woke up one day, and I realized I wanted a different life."

Pixie closed his eyes, disgusted with himself. There was a time he'd have completely understood Dane's thinking. The feeling of being trapped into a marriage, three kids, a mortgage, a club, all of it. Now, he didn't see it as a trap, but a fucking privilege.

"You walked away from one of the best women this world has to offer. She was there by your side when you fought. Through the losses and the wins, and I don't remember anyone ever pushing Lucy aside. She pushed them aside to get to you." Pixie shook his head. "She didn't want kids at the time, but she had them for you. The more I think about it, the more Lucy did for you, and you're just a selfish asshole."

"I never stopped loving her."

"But your dick was inside another woman."

"You fuck women every single day. All of them different."

"I'd never do that to the woman I commit the rest of my life to. That shit is sacred." He'd never cheat on Suzy. He loved her so much.

"No thanks, Chloe."

She didn't remember their names, but outside of the club, she rarely did. "Give me a call if you need anything."

Leaving the table, she took a quick second to catch her breath. She wasn't feeling too good, and it had started last night. Pressing a hand on her stomach, she closed her eyes and took another long deep breath. "It's fine."

"You okay?" Teri asked, calling through the serving hole.

"Yeah, I'm fine. You shouldn't be such a damn fine cook."

"I really am, aren't I?"

Chloe smiled, and got back to work. The hour rush drained her of any energy she had left. Entering the staffroom, she rushed toward the toilet, and stared at her reflection. She was getting really unfit. The sweat was pouring out of her.

Washing her face, and pressing a cool towel to the back of her neck, she released a little cough.

"Hot, so hot."

Once the buzzing stopped, and she was able to think once again, she took a deep breath, and made her way back outside toward the diners.

Grabbing the coffeepot she walked toward Grace and Drake.

"Hey, how was your vacation?" she asked.

"It was good. Wish one of you had called me to let me know that Dane was back," Drake said.

"He came back yesterday. We had no idea you were going to be back today," Chloe said.

"Yeah, this little guy wasn't feeling too good, and instead of tiring him out, we brought him back home."

Chloe smiled. "What can I get you?"

The door opened, and in walked Richard.

Her stomach twisted, and she no longer knew if it was a good or bad with the way she reacted to him.

"Teri's already dealing with our order," Drake said. "Are you okay?"

"Fine."

"You look really pale, and you're sweating."

"I'm fine. Really." She moved away and went to Richard's table. Being the successful lawyer he was, he rarely sat with the Dirty Fuckers MC. No one seemed to mind, but at times, she did.

"You didn't call me last night," he said.

After he took her home, he'd given her an instruction to phone him. It was mightily childish on her part, but she didn't want to follow his instructions. They were working on their issues, and she went away with him because he'd ordered her to. With Richard, he was always ordering her what to do, what to wear, what to say. He was willing to have her with him providing she looked and acted the part of his companion.

"I was tired."

She wiped at her brow and poured him out a coffee.

"Chloe, I would like you to move in with me."

She didn't even know how she felt about him, or if she even liked him.

"No," she said.

"I love you, Chloe."

Shaking her head, her stomach started to twist, and turn. "No, you don't." She took a step back, and collided with a chair. Unable to hold herself up, she fell back, spilling the hot coffee over her stomach.

"Chloe!"

She heard her name yelled, but she couldn't do anything. Her body ached, and she was so tired. Would it be so wrong to go to sleep?

Chapter Eight

Pixie stood in the hospital staring in at Chloe.

The entire club was in the hospital, and so was Suzy. What surprised everyone was the fact the next of kin on Chloe's form was listed as Suzy.

After collapsing in the diner, there had been no time for him to organize a vacation. Not only that, he didn't want to. The doctors didn't know what was wrong with her. They thought it was some kind of bug, so only Suzy could go in and see her.

Staring through the glass, Pixie saw the machines strapped up to Chloe, and he hated it. Richard paced up and down the hallway. Doctors, nurses, patients, hospital staff had tried to move them, but none of them were going anywhere. Chloe was one of them, and they were going to make sure she was looked after. They'd organized her private room, and let the good doctor know that if anything happened to her, it was him they were going to hold responsible.

"What the hell happened?" James asked.

"She was sweating," Drake said. Grace and Joseph had been there with them but since Chloe collapsed Drake had taken them home before coming to the hospital. "She looked ill, but she kept saying she was fine."

"I noticed her grabbing her stomach, or rubbing part of her body. There was pain, but when I asked, she always said she was fine," Teri said.

They were all worried for her.

Suzy came out of the room, and Pixie pulled her in his arms, hugging her. He didn't care what others thought. "She isn't talking, or responding."

"She's in a coma," Kitty said.

"I know. I just wished she'd talk back. It probably

sounds stupid, but it's not the same without her."

"We all get it," Cora said.

They were all here. The diner had been closed, and Cora called in a sick day. Even Lucy and Ryan had turned up. Chloe had touched a lot of people, Pixie included. She'd been a club whore, but she'd been the kind you actually enjoy having around.

Suzy rubbed at her eyes. "The doctor said they were running tests. It could be anything. An infection, meningitis, the flu, bird flu. I don't know."

"What was she like on your vacation?" James asked, turning toward Richard.

"Everything was great. We talked. We spent a lot of time together. She was healthy." Richard stared down at his hands. "I'm never going to get the image of her falling like that out of my head."

"She just collapsed," Drake said. "She stumbled over a chair, and it was like her body just gave way."

Pixie gripped Suzy's shoulder, needing comfort at hearing a friend was so ill. Damn, he liked Chloe.

She held onto his hand, locking their fingers together. The comfort of her touch was all he needed.

"How long do test results take?" Lucy asked.

Dane was in the hospital as well, and Pixie noticed he couldn't take his eyes off Lucy.

Too bad, buddy.

Pixie had imagined what would happen when Dane turned up. He always pictured greeting him with open arms, congratulating him on getting his balls back, taking what he wanted.

How time had changed him.

When Pixie looked at Dane, he didn't see a man. He saw a boy trapped in a man's body. The Dirty Fuckers MC had grown up. They were no longer children. They were fully grown men.

Pixie squeezed Suzy's hand.

The time for messing around, screwing everything in sight had long passed.

"Are you okay?"

"I'm fine. I just, I need some air."

"Let's go get some," Suzy said. "We'll be outside. Will you come and get me for the results?"

"Sure," James said.

They left the corridor, making their way out of the main hospital.

"What's wrong?" she asked.

The moment the cool air hit him, Pixie moved away and took several deep breaths. Pausing near a wall, he leaned forward, placing his hands on his knees, and closing his eyes.

"Pixie? Are you feeling ill, too?"

She pressed a hand to his forehead, but he shook his head. "No, I don't feel ill."

"What's wrong?"

"Everything."

Suzy didn't fight with him, or force him to explain himself.

"Shit, I'm sorry. I didn't mean to yell."

"It's okay."

"Everything is … shit. It's not shit. It's perfect, it really is perfect. Life is a grand old thing."

She frowned. "You're not making any sense right now."

"You know I've never cared about a single woman in my life." She didn't say anything. "Not one. There was my scarred brother, and me." He snorted. "I got the chicks, fucked them with him, and left them to be taken care of." Running fingers through his hair, he took a deep breath. "I didn't give a shit about them leaving my brother. If he even cared about them. The club, it has been a way for me to work without worrying about shit. James, he takes care of everything."

"Pixie."

"Leonard. It's my real name."

"I know."

"I used to believe life is just about living it. Settling down was for pussies who couldn't get a decent fuck, so they settled for the one thing. One hole their entire life. Sure, they change it up, pussy, ass, mouth, whatever they wanted to do to pretend it was really living." Pixie needed to get this off his chest. He needed for her to see that he was different. "Families were made to be ruined. They don't have any common ground. They fuck, push out some little brats, and they go off, or are sent off. When Dane came back married, I told him he'd live to regret it. There was more to life than Lucy's pussy."

"You're telling me everything you felt, past tense. Does that mean you've changed?" she asked.

He laughed. "Changed? Yeah, I've changed. I can't even stand to look at Dane without being angry. Cora and James, the love they have, I envy it. Fuck, everything I used to be, everything I stood for—I hate myself. I hate my own past thoughts. Knowing that I could have been the cause for Dane to leave, it sickens me. He cheated on her, you know."

"I don't know Dane or Lucy all that well."

"You'll like Lucy. She's got fire, like you, like your hair." He reached out, twirling a strand that had fallen out of her bun. "When I first met you, all I wanted to do was fuck you."

"And now?"

"I want to fuck you, always. But I don't want to ever let you go." He pulled her in close, breathing in her scent. "Sharing women never bothered me. They were easy to fuck, and when you shared, they were easier to leave. Two men, I could make my escape. The thought of anyone else touching you fills me with rage."

"I take it no sharing or ménage sex will be in my future."

"Never. I want you all to myself." He pulled away, cupping her face, and running his thumb across her lips. "What started out as a one-time deal is not what I want anymore," he said. "I want all of you, and more."

"I think the club knows we're together. If they didn't, they've got a pretty good idea now."

"I like that. I don't want to hide anymore. I love being with you, Suzy. I enjoy spending nights watching movies with you, spending the night, eating food, talking, walking, all of it."

She smiled. "Why, Leonard, you know how to charm a girl."

"Ugh, can we just stick with Pixie? I prefer it."

"I knew your name was Leonard, long before you started sleeping with me."

"How?"

"Last time I checked you couldn't put a nickname on a bank card. Every time you purchased something at the shop, you handed me your card. It didn't take long to figure out you were Leonard."

"I hate the name."

"I think it's cute." She smiled, and it took his breath away.

You're turning into a pussy.

"We better go in. I don't want to miss the doctor," she said.

"Why do you think she put you as the next of kin?" he asked.

"I imagine it's because we share an apartment. Chloe and I are close. Really close."

He liked that. Taking hold of her hand, they made their way up to the floor. Nothing had changed, apart from the fact everyone was drinking coffee.

They waited another hour before a tired, exhausted, and scruffy doctor came toward them. Pixie saw the man had been at the hospital for a long time.

"I'm so sorry it has taken me this long to get back to you," he said.

"It's okay. What's wrong with Chloe?"

****

Encephalitis was what was wrong with Chloe. They had already started pumping her with medication, and were keeping 'round the clock care. They wouldn't know for certain of the damage until she woke up.

Suzy had never been so happy to hear such a diagnosis. She'd been freaking out. Before Pixie's big revelation when she was sitting in the hospital, talking with Chloe, she'd tried to figure out what was wrong. Talking to Chloe, asking questions, getting no response. At first she'd been worried in case Fluffy had given her something. In the end, it had been an infection that hadn't been treated, but had gotten worse. It was common, treatable, but also dangerous.

Sitting in Chloe's room now, Suzy told her the good news.

"Everyone was here a second ago. After the diagnosis, James gave a lot of instructions. Several of the guys are going to be here, and we're going to take care of you." She touched Chloe's hand, giving it a squeeze. "You scared us there for a second. Well, you scared me. Teri was pretty damn petrified, and you know how much steel she has." She chuckled. "It's official now. I'm dating Pixie, and when you get out, and are well again, we may be going away on a vacation together." She licked her lips. "I even think we're going to be boyfriend and girlfriend. Do you know how weird that sounds? I've never had a boyfriend. It has always been Pixie. All of my firsts are with him." In the private room she heard the beeping of the machines. Hospitals always made her uncomfortable. "You scared me, Chloe. I like having you around. You're funny, witty, and I love you, sweetie." She stared at the woman on the bed. Chloe was a beautiful woman, inside and out. She deserved so much love, and happiness.

"Is she awake?" Pixie asked, popping his head around the door.

She turned toward him. "Not yet."

He entered the room, even though he wasn't allowed. "You're talking to her?"

"Always. The doctor said her vitals were looking good."

"You need to go home," he said. "It's getting late."

Her stomach chose that time to grumble. "Who will sit with her?"

"I will," James said, entering the room. He carried a book. "I'll take care of her."

"Taking care of people is what you do best, brother."

"I try. I wish I could say that I did a good job."

"I've just been talking to her," Suzy said, standing up. "You'll call the moment she wakes up, right?"

"Of course. I wouldn't hide it." James smiled down at Chloe. "She's had everyone worried about her."

"See you in the morning if she hasn't woken up by then," Pixie said.

They were at the door when James called to them.

"I'm glad you two have decided to come out with your relationship. It's nothing to be ashamed of, falling for each other."

Pixie gripped her shoulders, and she had to wonder if he regretted his decision to let everyone know what was happening.

"Thank you," she said.

They left the hospital, saying goodbye to Leo and Paul on the way out.

Suzy climbed into the passenger seat of Pixie's car, her stomach doing another grumble.

"Do you want me to stop off for food?"

"No, I can make us something back at the apartment." She pulled her bun out, and ran her fingers through her hair. "I feel so achy."

"I hope you're not coming down with it."

"No. I think it's because I've sat down in the same position for a long time. My body is protesting."

The drive back to her place was uneventful. Entering her apartment, Fluffy was barking, and spinning around. Before she picked him up, Pixie was there. "I think this little guy is hungry."

"Yeah, I'll get him some food. I've already taken him for a walk." Fluffy was house-trained, and only required small walking three times a day.

Leaving Fluffy with Pixie, she grabbed his empty bowl, washing it before putting some more food into it.

Pixie was dancing around with the dog in his arms, and Suzy paused, watching him. If someone had told her a year ago this would be her life, she'd have laughed at them. Pixie in her apartment, dancing with her dog seemed so out of place.

"He likes you."

"Good. I like him."

She laughed. Putting his bowl down, she watched as Pixie lowered Fluffy to the floor, and the dog ran toward his food.

"One hungry guy fed, how about you, big boy?" she asked.

"I'll take some food."

Entering the kitchen once again, she grabbed several pans, putting them on the stove. Chicken fettuccine alfredo it was. With Pixie watching her, she seasoned the chicken, searing it in the pan until lovely and golden. In another pot of water, she dumped the pasta.

Within twenty minutes, they were eating the creamy sauce.

"I'm pleased nothing bad happened to Chloe," he said.

"You and me both." She had noticed that when it came to Pixie's feelings he was rather childlike in his approach. It was strange, but she imagined Pixie had never really talked about his feelings, or cared about it.

Once she finished with dinner, they did the dishes together, and then went to her bedroom. Without waiting for him to avert his gaze, she removed her clothes, dumping them in the laundry basket. Tomorrow was laundry day. It was Chloe's turn, but Grace would do it. They didn't have a washing machine in the apartment, so they always had to go downstairs to get their laundry done.

"I'm going to take a shower," she said. Entering her bathroom, she turned the shower on, giving it time to heat up. Standing beneath the spray, she tilted her head up, closing her eyes.

Seconds passed before she felt Pixie behind her. "You didn't say I couldn't join you."

She smiled. "I figured you would. We want to save the environment, shower together."

"I think that's a good way to be." He reached past her, taking the soap. She watched as he covered his hands, and then placed them on her body. He cupped her tits, massaging her nipples. "We can start here." He ran his hands over her tits, pinching the hard buds, and stroking out any pain that he might have caused. "I love your tits. I love how big they are."

"Pixie," she said, moaning his name.

"Are you wet for me?"

"Yes."

He rinsed his hands and glided them down her body, going over her rounded stomach to rest between her thighs. He slid a finger between her folds, and this time he moaned. "You're always so wet for me."

"It's how you make me feel."

"I make you feel good, don't I, baby?"

"Always."

He slid a finger inside her, and she opened her thighs wide. "You want me to fuck you?"

"Yes."

"First, you're going to come all over my hand."

As he slid two fingers inside her, his thumb stroked over her clit. She cried out his name, wishing it was his dick inside her as he stroked her to release.

"I feel your cunt, baby, it's begging for me, begging for my dick. Do you want it?"

"Yes, please, yes, I want it."

He spun her around, pressed her up against the tile wall, and lifted her up. It always amazed her how easily he lifted her. To him, it was like she had no weight, when she knew the truth.

Wrapping her legs around his waist, she gasped as he thrust deep inside her, filling her.

"Fuck, so tight. Always so tight."

She wrapped her arms around his neck, holding him tightly as he started to fuck her. Pixie took his time at first, driving in and out of her. She wanted him to go deeper, to take her so completely.

Pixie wouldn't be rushed. He took his time, making love to her.

When she couldn't stand it anymore, he started to fuck her harder. There was no need to contain her sounds, and the freedom to finally be with him liberated her.

"Yes, please, please. Oh my God, Pixie."

He drove her to orgasm. She clutched him tightly as he found his own release.

Chapter Nine

With Chloe being in the hospital, Lucy expected Dane to come and visit her. It wasn't a surprise when later that night the doorbell rang. She'd changed the locks years ago when he first left. With three kids, she didn't want to risk their safety just because she thought he was coming back.

Opening the door, she stared at the man that no longer resembled her husband. The man she had once loved with all of her heart was gone. The only clue to her that Dane had been that man was his eyes. She'd loved staring into his eyes, and it had been the first thing that enthralled her about him all those years back in Vegas.

Dane, the man she loved, hadn't been so muscular, or covered with as many tattoos. He rarely grew facial hair either. Their son, Ryan, resembled the young Dane so much. This man though, she didn't know him.

"Can I come in?" he asked.

She opened the door and turned toward the kitchen.

The youngest two were asleep, but Ryan was in his room. She didn't know if he'd heard the door, or if he'd even want to talk to his father. Dane leaving had really screwed with Ryan's head, and with her heart.

"You don't seem surprised to see me."

"Chloe's in the hospital. James took over, and he gave everyone instructions. He's the most consistent guy out of all the club, and I guessed he'd be taking the night shift. You don't become a priority anymore." She put the kettle on, grabbing them out two cups. "Say what you want to say."

"I'm not signing the divorce."

"Why not?"

"I don't want to divorce you."

She laughed. "You're priceless."

"I love you, Lucy."

She spun around, glaring at the man that had ripped her heart out, and stomped on it. "No, you don't. You never really did."

"Lucy."

"No. I want a divorce. I don't want to be married to you. I haven't wanted to be married to you for a long time. The club tried looking for you. Did you know that?"

"I figured they would."

"Good old Dane. He'll be found when he wants to be found. You didn't want to be found though, did you? No, he wanted to stay away, and pretend he was something he wasn't." She finished making them a cup of tea.

Lucy's voice didn't rise, didn't change an octave as she spoke to him. When she realized that he was first gone, she had been completely and utterly broken. He'd left her, abandoned her. Three kids, a mortgage, bills, debts, everything had fallen to her. Dane had promised to take care of her. In the end, he nearly ruined her.

"What did you do with your time? What did you do with your newfound freedom?" she asked.

"I thought about you every day."

She let out a breath. "No, you didn't."

"Lucy?"

"No." She handed him a coffee. "You don't get to sit there and pretend that you did something. If you cared, you'd have called. If you cared, you'd have given me some warning. You left me all alone, Dane. Don't even try to tell me that you stayed faithful either. I know you too well."

She watched as he averted his gaze, confirming

her suspicions. He hadn't been faithful to her. Dane had left her with three kids.

"You never kept your promise to me. The least you can do is sign the damn paperwork releasing me from you."

****

"I promise to never break your heart. To love you for all of my life. I'll be there for you always. You don't have to rely on anyone else. I'll be there."

Dane had promised Lucy that on the day he proposed. She had wanted to wait, but he'd insisted that they marry sooner rather than later. She wanted to wait for kids, but he'd knocked her up as soon as he could.

Once they had three kids, and life was on track, it had been too much for him, and he bolted.

He hadn't been faithful to her.

There had been countless women over the past few years. Young, old, fat, thin, He hadn't cared. He had fucked them because in that moment, he'd been single. The ring he wore had been on the necklace tied around his neck.

It had been a game to him, making up for lost time.

"I heard you found someone," he said.

"I have. He's a good man. I love him."

Dane had never expected her admission to hurt. Not only did it hurt, it cut him deep.

She gripped the edge of the island that he had once installed.

"You once loved me."

"I love the man that wouldn't have left me. The man that wouldn't cheat on me. You're not that man."

"I'm still me."

"No. I wouldn't even trust you anymore."

"None of us would," Ryan said, making them

turn toward the door. Dane stared at his son, and his heart broke a little more. Ryan was no longer a little boy. He was a man, struggling with his temper, channeling his rage into his fists.

"Are you okay?" Lucy asked.

"Yeah, Mom, I'm fine. I want to know why you have him here."

"I'm hoping he can sign the divorce papers."

"You tell him everything now?" Dane asked.

"She's my mom, of course she does." Ryan went to the fridge, and Dane realized how much of an outsider he was. This was his son, his wife, and he had two other kids upstairs.

While you'd been fucking your way through each state, your family had been here.

"Lewis is a good man. He loves Mom."

"You want me to divorce your mother?"

"Why not? You left without a word. You could have been dead, and it would be no different from a divorce." Ryan shrugged. "You know, I was angry with you for leaving, and now I'm angry at you for being back." He shook his head. "I used to think you were the shit."

"Ryan?"

"No, Mom, I won't be silent anymore. I've hurt people who didn't need to be hurt. I pushed my anger everywhere else but at the person it needed to be directed at." Ryan stared Dane in the eyes. "I hate you. I don't want you in my life, and I wish you were dead."

With that, Ryan left the kitchen.

"I think we need to talk about this some more," Dane said.

"You need to go," Lucy said.

Nodding, he didn't see a reason to argue. Getting to his feet, he made his way toward the door. When he made to kiss Lucy's cheek, she jerked away from him. "No."

Everything was falling apart. Dane had never expected this to happen. He'd always assumed that Lucy and his life would be waiting for him. Who would want a woman with three kids?

He was an asshole.

Dane had lost the woman he once loved, and there was no chance of him ever winning her back.

****

The following day Chloe woke up from her coma. She was still sick, and being intravenously fed the medication, but she was awake. The doctor wouldn't let her go for a couple more days, maybe even up to a week.

"Do you have any idea how much you scared me?" Suzy asked.

"You're just worried in case you had to pay the rest of the rent."

Suzy chuckled. "Yeah, totally, that was my main concern. How would I pay the rent?" She rolled her eyes. Leaning forward, she wrapped her arms around her friend, holding her close. "I love you, you know that."

"I know that."

"You scared the hell out of us," Pixie said.

They had already brought Chloe up to speed, letting her know about their relationship.

"Richard's outside," Suzy said.

"He is?"

"Yeah, he was here." Suzy reached out, pushing some hair off her face. "You put me down as the next of kin."

"I know. It made sense to me. I was living in the apartment with you. Why wouldn't you be my next of kin?"

"It was kind of weird having to make decisions

for you. I just wanted to force you to wake up to tell me what to do. We'll have to have a talk about that."

"We're getting serious, Suzy. Relationship standard."

"Don't talk to me about relationships. I'm entering uncharted territory. I'm frightened."

Chloe laughed. "You'll do great."

"Do you want to talk to Richard?" Suzy asked.

She sighed. "I must have scared him half to death, face-planting the floor."

"You tripped over a chair. You're going to have some bruising on your body."

Chloe sighed. "I've had worse."

"You've asked for worse," Suzy said, smirking.

"You're good for the soul, did you know that?"

"I should put that on all future friendship applications. Benefit of befriending Suzy, she's an awesome friend."

"And an awesome girlfriend," Pixie said.

"Am I going to be grossed out by you two?" Chloe asked. "Do I need to go apartment hunting?"

"No," they both said in unison.

"No apartment hunting," Suzy said. "Pixie may be staying over sometimes."

Chloe nodded. "I'm getting tired. I hate to push you out, but I need—"

"You need rest. Don't say any more." Suzy jumped up out of her seat. "We're not going away until you're back home, and well."

"I'll hurry," Chloe said.

"No, no need to hurry, take your time."

Chloe watched them leave, and made herself sit up. She was still so tired, and her body ached all over.

"You're not going to invite me in?" Richard asked.

She looked toward the door, seeing him carrying a large bouquet of roses. "Wow, they're huge."

"I want you to get well soon."

"They're beautiful." Chloe saw they already had a vase and water. "You prepare for everything, don't you?"

"Of course. Only a fool does things by halves."

She didn't know why she was so nervous around him. It was Richard, a man she had slept with. A man she loved, and yet, she couldn't shake the nerves that filled her when he was near.

"You didn't have to stay at the hospital. I know how busy you are."

"I'll never be too busy for you, Chloe."

He stood at the base of her bed, his hands gripping the railing. The suit he wore did nothing to hide the thick muscles of his arms.

She licked her lips.

"What is it?" he asked.

"Nothing."

"I didn't even realize you were sick."

"Don't worry about it. *I* didn't realize I was sick."

"I'm supposed to know."

She shook her head. "You're not God, Richard."

"I'm the man who is supposed to care for you."

Chloe leaned back, feeling exhausted. "I'm fine, and soon I'll be well."

He moved, taking a seat on the bed. "What is going on with us, Chloe?"

"I don't know."

"When we were at the club, we connected. You were so attuned to me, and I knew what you were thinking, feeling, all of it. What's going on?"

She licked her dry lips. "When I'm with you, I don't feel like I belong."

"Of course you do."

She smiled. "It doesn't matter."

Richard went to say something, and then stopped. A nurse came in and started to check on her vitals.

"We'll talk another time," he said.

He didn't leave the room though. Richard took a seat, and Chloe lay down. Tired, she fell to sleep.

****

When Suzy wasn't visiting Chloe at the hospital, or working for James, Pixie had her all to himself. He loved not having to hide his feelings for her. The club still had a lot of business to deal with, like making a decision about Dane. Was he going to remain part of the club, or were they going to get rid of him? Pixie wanted him gone. He'd seen the damage the man had done to his family.

The Dirty Fuckers MC was a club, a brotherhood of pleasure, but Dane had walked away. He caused pain not only to the club, but to a woman and children.

James wasn't in the right mood to discuss Dane. With Chloe in the hospital, regular business deals, his brother was swamped. Suzy helped though. She took a huge weight off his shoulders by dealing with all of the paperwork.

"Do you even own a place of your own?" Suzy asked.

He'd entered James's office at five, and lured her out with the promise of food and sex. Food being the first point, sex being the latter.

There was a scene occurring in the private room between some close friends of the club. Eric Wiseman was a friend, along with his wife, Tory. They had high-powered jobs, each one a CEO of a company. Both of them came to the club from the city for some down time, and with it, a chance to play.

Eric was a Dom and Tory a submissive. The club was open to them, to play, to scene, and to have the security that their identities would remain a secret.

After feeding Suzy, Pixie took her hand, and led her toward the private playroom. He'd wanted for her to see Caleb in action. Now she would have to watch Eric. Pixie wasn't a Dom. He wouldn't dare use any of the equipment on a woman, but he liked to watch. He hoped Suzy found the same enjoyment from watching as he did.

"We're here again," she said, whispering the words to him.

"We're here, and you've got nothing to fear." He pressed a kiss to her lips.

"They're not Caleb and Kitty."

"I know. This is another couple."

"Do you want to do this? You and me?"

"No. I wouldn't even know where to start. I just like to watch."

"Oh. A little voyeur inside you."

"Always." He pulled her against him, and they settled back to watch the show.

Suzy had seen stuff on the internet, but it was never this personal. It was almost next to impossible in this day and age to miss something like this. Everywhere she turned, everything was sex oriented.

The guy, Eric, wasn't as big as Pixie. He was a businessman, that she saw easily enough. In front of Eric was a woman. She was small, slender to the point that her hip bones showed. Glancing up at Pixie, Suzy wondered if that was what he liked. Did he hate her curves?

Don't be stupid.

Pixie hadn't given her any sign that he didn't love her body. In fact, every chance he got, he showed that he adored her and her curves.

Settling back against him, she watched as the man ran his fingers across the woman's shoulders into her hair. Eric whispered something, and the woman turned, presenting him with her back.

Suzy watched as he held her hair, and began to plait the long blonde tresses down her back. He finished it off with a band that feel at the base of her ass.

"I'll never know how he learned to do that," Pixie said, whispering.

They couldn't hear what was being said, but Suzy didn't need to hear. She saw the love, the contentment, and also the trust between the couple. Tory turned back toward Eric, and the kiss between them was explosive.

Pixie took her hand, and she smiled. She loved it when they touched. Locking her fingers with his, she released a breath, smiling as she stared at the couple.

"What do you need?" Eric asked.

"I need to be punished, Sir. I was late every single day last week, and you had told me not to be."

"You want me to punish you?"

"I need it."

"Do you trust me?"

"Completely."

Eric pressed a kiss to her cheek. "Let's begin."

She watched transfixed as Tory sank to the floor. Her knees were spread, and even though she was naked, Tory didn't try to cover up. Her hands rested with her palms up. Her head slightly bent, and from seeing submissive artwork on the net, Suzy knew it was the ultimate submissive pose.

Eric stood back and nodded. "Very good, my beauty. Seeing you like this, I know you belong totally to me."

"Eric is very possessive. He won't let anyone else touch Tory. It's difficult for him to let her go to work, knowing men will be drooling over her," Pixie said.

"Do you drool over her?"

"No. I admire their relationship. You can't deny they have something going on."

She couldn't deny it. Suzy couldn't look away. It was seeing a view of two people, a couple, that she truly believed she'd never get to see.

Eric requested Tory's hand, and he helped the woman to stand.

Suzy waited as he pulled her in close, slamming his lips against hers. All the time, Suzy felt Pixie right beside her. The emotions she watched pass between the Dom and his submissive were not the same, and yet they were for how she felt about Pixie. Eric ran his hands over Tory's body, stroking each part of her. Tory didn't fight. She accepted every touch, every pinch, and slap.

When it came time to the main punishment, Suzy saw how desperate Tory was. The other woman was practically giddy with excitement. If that hadn't been confirmed with her bouncing body, then it was confirmed with her pussy.

Even though Suzy was uncomfortable with seeing another woman's arousal, she couldn't help but see why Tory was so turned on. It wasn't just about the punishment either. Tory clearly loved and respected Eric.

Suzy watched as Eric started slowly, using his hands. He'd slap Tory's ass, lightly, then hard. The moment he struck her hard, he'd soothe out the pain, running his fingers across the marks. Tory's ass was a lovely shade of pink before he moved up to a whip. Suzy tensed up, but as Eric struck, Tory moaned.

The scene built as Eric struck Tory. She begged and pleaded for more. Throughout it all, Eric stroked her body, constantly checking if she was okay. If Tory was showing any signs of the scene going too far, he'd calm down, resorting to his hand rather than an actual piece of equipment.

When the spanking was done, he'd tease her with toys, moving her body, strapping her down as he brought her to a sweat with everything he did her. Once the punishment was over, Suzy watched as Eric finally claimed his woman.

To Suzy, it no longer felt dirty. If anything, it was a privilege to watch this couple, and to see something that she would like as well. She didn't want to be tied up or spanked, or dominated in such a way. No, what she wanted was the same feelings that Tory had for Eric. The connection, the love, and above all the respect and trust. That was what a relationship was about, and that was what Suzy hoped to have one day with Pixie.

Eric picked Tory up in his arms, and Pixie urged Suzy out of the booth, and they left the couple to finish what they needed.

"Wow," she said when they were in private. "I see why it's so magical to watch."

"It really is. Eric and Tory, that was quite tame to some of the stuff I've seen them do. I don't want to do it. I just like watching."

She smiled. "You don't have to worry." Moving toward him, she wrapped her arms around his neck. "I like this."

"What?"

"Being able to touch you without fear of someone else coming in, and having to let go."

"You could always touch me, baby. That was never in question."

She released a sigh. "You're too good for me, Pixie." He looked away, and she frowned at the troubled look on his face. "What's wrong?"

"Nothing. Forget it."

"You can tell me."

"I know. It's nothing."

She decided to let it go. The last thing she wanted to do was spoil a night because he was worried about something. It was probably Chloe, or maybe something to do with the club. She didn't know.

He'd tell her when he was ready.

****

James stared down at some of Suzy's notes. Hiring that woman had actually been a godsend. She knew how to organize paperwork, and even though it was still going to take some time, she'd done a huge chunk of it already.

There was even a chance he wouldn't have to hire someone for a week to come and deal with his taxes. His world was good. Cora was meeting him at the diner, and they were going to share a meal there before heading home.

With the worry for Chloe, James had not been able to be with his woman. However, it had highlighted some concerns, and he wanted to talk to Cora about them.

When someone cleared his throat, James looked up.

Dane stood in his office doorway, holding some paperwork.

"What's the matter?" James asked.

"I spoke with Lucy a few days ago."

"I figured you would. I didn't realize that I'd not dealt with you until it was too late. Those the divorce papers?"

"Yes. She wants nothing from me. The house, it was in her name anyway at the bank. I just deposited the money into the account to pay for it."

"Which you stopped doing when you went away

for your own reasons."

Dane dropped his head. "I fucked up, and I'm finally seeing how much."

"I take it Lucy won't retract the divorce?"

"No. She wants the divorce, and she wants absolutely nothing to do with me. Neither does my own son. Ryan sure has grown."

"Like I said, you hurt him. You hurt everyone by leaving. We all tried to find you."

"I have a knack for not being found."

James shrugged. "Again, that was your doing, not ours. We tried to find you. Not just for the club, or for Lucy, but for your kids. They don't trust you now."

"No. They trust this Lewis guy. I was in the diner when Lucy, the kids, and this mystery guy turned up. I was so fucking angry, so jealous. He had no right touching my woman, and then it was like a switch went off inside my head. When I was screwing all those fucking road bunnies, I didn't give a thought to Lucy, or my life, or anything else."

"Do you want to give a shit now?"

"I don't want to leave town. I don't want to leave the club. I've signed the divorce papers, and I will do everything I have to do. I want to make this right." Dane handed over the papers, and James saw the signature.

"We're going to need to take a vote."

Dane held his hand up. "I understand. I let everyone down." He sighed. "Even if you vote me out, I'm not leaving. I'll earn my patch again if I have to. I fucked up once. I'm not going to fuck up again."

During dinner with Cora, James told her about the meeting.

"What do you want to do?"

"I want to kick his ass out."

"Is that as a club prez, or is that because he left

his wife and kids?" Cora asked, stealing a fry from his plate.

"I think it's a mixture of both. He was a good guy. Fought like a fucking fiend, like the depths of hell was chasing him. Up until this moment I'd say he was loyal as fuck."

"Now?"

"I don't know." James ran a hand over his face. "I really don't know what to do with him. The club needs to vote on it."

"I heard Leo and Paul saying that they couldn't trust him anymore. They wouldn't be surprised if he ran or something."

"See, and that is why I don't know what's going to happen." James sighed. "We're not a conventional club, Cora. We don't run drugs, guns, or shit."

"You fuck, I get it. The Dirty Fuckers MC and all." She smiled. "I happen to know that their prez is one hot piece in the sack."

James chuckled. "You bet your hot ass I am. There's something else I want to talk to you about."

"This sounds serious."

"I know we're not married, and neither of us need a piece of paper to know that we're married in real life."

She covered his hand. "This is about Chloe, isn't it?"

"Yeah."

"I was thinking the same thing. If anything was to happen to me, I'd like to know you're safe," she said, surprising him.

"About me being safe?"

"Hello, the house is all in my name. I pay the mortgage, babe. I want that house to go to you, and to our kids when we have them."

"You see us having kids?" James asked.

"Don't you? I know we're not in a rush, but I want to be a mother one day. I won't be the conventional mother, standing at the stove, making her own medicine, and telling kids how to make the best apple pie."

James burst out laughing. No, their kids wouldn't have that, but they'd have Cora. Her loyalty and heart were worth a lot more than that.

"Marriage in a way protects that. It protects us, and it will protect you. It'll mean you've got what I own, and so do our children." Cora grabbed his hand. "Are you afraid yet?"

"Not a chance. I'm just trying to wonder who won what today? Neither of us wanted a big lavish wedding or shit."

"Then let's not. Let's just go down to the town hall with a license, and get married. That's it."

"Is that what you want?" he asked.

"Yeah. I have you. I don't care about anything else. We're doing this to secure our futures for each other. Also, if you ever, and I mean ever, leave me, and cheat on me the way Dane did Lucy, I will hunt you down, cut your dick off, and make you wish you'd never looked in another woman's direction. Clear?"

"God, I love you, woman."

Chapter Ten

One week later

Suzy rolled over and smiled as Pixie lay still asleep. Chloe had returned home two days ago, and yesterday they'd spent most of the day traveling. He'd booked them at this beautiful beach resort, in a secluded bay near the ocean. They didn't get the chance to admire the beauty around them as it had been dark when they landed.

"Hey, beautiful," he said, reaching out to stroke her cheek.

"I thought you were asleep."

"I was. I love that smile on your pretty face." He ran his thumb across her lip.

She bit his thumb, and giggled as he released a moan. Moving over him, she straddled his waist. "Are you ready to go out today?"

He gripped her hips, and moved her so that his cock was right next to her pussy.

"Baby, I can think of much more thrilling ways to spend the first morning."

"Me too." She pulled her nightshirt off over her head and then moved over him. He took one of her nipples into his mouth, and sucked the bud deep inside, making her moan.

Holding the foil packet like it was victory, she held it up for him to see. "Ready?"

"Yes. I'm ready." Suddenly he hesitated.

"What is it? Do you want me to get off?"

"No. No, it's fine." He took the condom from her and tore into the packet. She moved out of the way, watching as he rolled the latex down his cock.

Taking hold of his hands, she followed his direction, and lowered herself onto his cock. They both moaned as he sank deep inside her. Closing her eyes, she squeezed her pussy, feeling him jerk deep within her. "You don't know how much I love it when you fucking do that."

Lifting up, she slammed herself back down on his cock, taking him deeper inside.

Pixie let go of her hands, grabbing her hips, and took control, showing her how hard he wanted it, and how deep he wanted to go. She loved every second of his control as he took charge.

When she didn't think she could stand anymore, he rolled her over, and they ended up on the floor with him still inside her. Pixie reared back, grabbed her ass, and slammed all the way inside her, going as deep as he could possibly go. Suzy stared up into his eyes, and just knew without a shadow of a doubt that this man belonged to her, and she did with him.

They were meant to be together.

Over the past year Pixie had worked his way into her heart, and there was no way of letting him go, not now, not ever. He'd showed her a different side of himself, and she loved it.

Riding his cock, she reached between them, and fingered her pussy, seeing it drive him over the edge. They came together, screaming each other's name as bliss completely took over. Afterward, he collapsed over her, and she ran her hands down his shoulders, the tattoos standing out against his skin.

"You're so utterly beautiful," he said.

"I don't want this to end."

"Me neither."

"How about some sunbathing?" she asked.

"You read my mind."

After a quick shower together, Suzy dressed into a bathing suit with a sarong wrapped around her hips.

Pixie wore a pair of shorts, nothing else. She pushed her sunglasses up into her hair, and waited as he put a call through to James. They hadn't gotten the time last night to let the club know they had arrived safely.

Holding hands, they made their way toward the beach. He carried some towels, and when they found a good spot, he placed them on the sand.

Sitting beside him, she noticed the beach was filling up with people.

"I've got some lotion. Turn around, let me do your back," he said.

"I have to say I'm surprised we went away alone together. I thought we'd end up in some hotel in a city." She gasped as the cool lotion touched her skin.

"Is that because of the club?"

"Partly. You don't really do much without each other. Isn't it for protection or something?"

"If I was going to another area where a club is predominantly known I'd have needed to ask permission, and then I wouldn't have stayed in that location. Some clubs are real fucking assholes when it comes to marking their territory. I'm sure they've pissed over everything if they could."

She burst out laughing. "I take it you don't like some clubs."

"Not like, but I'd never want to be on vacation near them. Some clubs I've heard about fucking attract trouble."

"Like who?"

"The Skulls being one. They're a club, a fucking dangerous one, out near Fort Wills. Believe it or not, they're closely linked to Ned Walker as well."

"Ned Walker? Who is he?"

"Like a fighting legend. He's got balls of steel, and even being as old as he is, I wouldn't go up against him. Fucker has friends in high places. I imagine the day someone takes him out, they're going to have a shitload of problems on their hands."

She couldn't help the shiver of fear. "Are you in danger?"

"Not really. Dirty Fuckers don't meddle in the kind of business some clubs do. The most dangerous thing we ever did was fight. All of us, and of course we've picked up a few strays along the way." He shrugged. "Like you, my darling."

"You consider me a stray."

"Well, you're helping to tame this monster right here."

He turned her around, and then started to massage the cream into her chest. "Stop that. We're on a beach with kids. You can have your little private session when we get back."

"Damn, and here I was hoping for some rough fucking with the sand."

"So you can be washing sand out of all of those hard-to-reach places?" she asked.

"Totally. It'll remind me all the time of our precious fuck session."

Rolling her eyes, she rested her head on his shoulder. She really did enjoy being with him. Pulling away, she took the lotion from his hand, and urged him to move so she could do his back as well.

Squirting some of the cool lotion on his back, she ran her hands over the impressive expanse of hard, inked muscles. She noticed several women admiring her man, and she did her best to ignore them. They were not going to spoil her trip, or her fun.

Running her hands all over his back, at the same time he rubbed it into his chest. Once they were done, he lay back. "I intend to burn to a crisp."

She smiled, rolling onto her stomach, and grabbing her book.

"Read to me."

Starting at the top of the page, she read the book to him, waiting for him to make a comment. Yes, she liked erotic fiction. She found it far more enjoyable than anything else.

"I have to say I'm scandalized. You're reading a naughty book on the beach." He rolled over, and leaned in close. "You can read about anal, but you can't have it done?"

"It's different."

"Why?"

"I'm reading about it here, not actually doing it." They weren't close to anyone so she didn't mind talking about it with him.

"I have to say I'm a little disappointed."

She smiled. "You're disappointed with everything."

"Actually, baby, I'm not. I love your perfect pussy, and your precious mouth. I've taken all of your virgin parts, so let me have this virgin part as well." He placed a hand on her ass, and she rolled her ass.

"What virgin part do I have?" she asked.

"First of all, you have me, and the fact I'm not with anyone else. That, in itself, is a virgin of something. They can call oil fucking virgin and extra-virgin, I can call our relationship a virgin."

She laughed, shaking her head.

"The way I feel about you. It's new to me."

"How do you feel?" she asked.

"Like I'm on top of the world when I'm with you. When I'm with you, I want to know what you're thinking, what you're feeling. Your hopes, your dreams, your desires. I want to live every single one of your fantasies out, and they don't even have to be about sex either."

"They don't?"

"No. You want to go out to a posh restaurant, spend thousands on a meal Teri can do better, I'd do it for you."

She touched his cheek. "I don't need anything but you."

"So, the virgin ass thing."

"I'll think about it." She leaned over and kissed her.

Suddenly a shadow fell over them, and they pulled apart to look up at two women. Suzy saw their slender bodies in the revealing bikinis. They were with a bunch of other women, and a few men. They'd been watching Pixie with hunger in their eyes since the moment they got there.

"Can I help you?" Pixie asked.

"Yes, would your sister mind if we borrow you for a little while? We're going to play some volleyball, and the guys need a big strapping man like you."

One of the women cocked her hip and stared hungrily at him.

"Sorry, ladies. I'm with my woman, and she's not my sister. Find some other poor sap to abuse. I'm happy with the woman I've got." Suzy didn't get to say anything as Pixie took possession of her lips, and let them know the last thing she was, was his sister. "Cheeky bitches, thinking you were my sister. Not that I have a sister, but I can promise you I never want to fuck James's ass."

She burst out laughing. "You're really bad, you know that."

"I try."

****

The week went by too fast for Pixie. They divided their time between the beach, walking around the island, and spending time alone in bed. He loved having her all to himself, and he also gave her a ban on clothes. Pixie loved seeing her naked, and knowing no one was going to interrupt them.

At the beginning of the week, he'd been so pissed with those girls at the beach. Calling Suzy his sister, he'd seen her instant withdrawal, and it only served to piss him off. How dare they treat her like that? He'd soon showed them, and he wouldn't be without her by his side.

Every single day his feelings grew deeper, and to Pixie he knew without a shadow of a doubt that he loved her. He loved her more than anything in the world, and late one night, he had to call James. He didn't care about the time.

The only person he wanted to talk to was his brother. James was thrilled but also asked what Suzy thought of his feelings.

He'd been stumped.

This week had been about trying to get her to fall in love with him, and obviously to see how his feelings were. There was no doubt for him. Suzy was the one woman he'd been waiting for.

And you're already lying to her.

Staring down at the sleeping face, he pushed some hair out of her face. He'd done a really bad thing. An awful thing, and just thinking about it, made him feel a little sick.

She didn't know what he'd done, and when he looked at the drawer beside their bed, he saw the evidence in the condoms he'd bought from home. The condoms he'd pierced so that he had a reason to protect her.

You're a fucking idiot.

Damn, fuck, damn.

She trusted him, and he saw that.

The trust would be destroyed if she ever found out.

Now he was torn between telling her the truth, and also ruining whatever chance they had.

Fuck!

Fuck, fuck, fuck, fuck, fuck.

"What's the matter, baby?" she said, opening her eyes, and smiling at him.

"What?"

"You kept saying the word fuck."

"I said that out loud?"

She nodded, humming. "Yes."

"It's nothing. I was just thinking about you, and of course that's what I think at the same time."

"I love it when you make me smile, and you make me smile all the time, Pixie." She rolled over, cupping his cheek. Lifting up, she pressed a kiss to his lips. "You're so patient with me, and I love our vacation."

"We're heading home soon."

"Yes, we are." She rolled away from him again, and grabbed something out of a drawer. "I noticed you packed this." She held up the kit he'd wanted to use on her in the apartment.

His cock went from flaccid to rock hard within a second.

"Would you still like to use it?"

"Fuck, yeah."

Taking the kit from her hand, he cupped her cheeks, and kissed her lips. He loved this woman. He loved her kind heart, her adventurous nature even when she was scared, and every other part in between.

"I want to give you everything you've ever wanted," she said.

He deepened the kiss, trying to show her with actions rather than words exactly how he felt about her. Sliding his hand down her naked body, he cupped her breast, fingering the nipple before moving to the next. She arched up against him. He didn't break the kiss, continuing to tease her body.

Moving between her spread legs, he found her pussy slick and her clit swollen. He moaned as did she when he slid a finger deep within her. Her pussy tightened around his finger as he pumped it inside her.

"Please, Pixie," she said, pulling away long enough to beg him.

"You want to come?"

"Yes, God yes."

He pulled his fingers out of her pussy, trailing them back to her anus. He moved her onto her stomach, and helped her to her knees.

"I want you to trust me."

"Okay."

Using the lube from her pussy, he circled his fingers against her anus, preparing her ass for the fake cock's invasion. Opening the kit with one hand, he pulled the tube of lubrication out, and using his teeth, undid the cap. Squirting a generous amount onto his fingers, he pushed one digit inside her, going past the tight ring of muscles. In and out he worked his finger until he was able to press in a second.

She didn't fight him, and he was satisfied. He pulled his fingers from her ass and grabbed the fake cock from the kit. Applying lube, he took his time inserting the cock into her ass. Each whimper, her stopped, and stroked her body, bringing her arousal higher. Only when he was satisfied that she was ready, did he push the cock a little deeper inside her.

"How does it feel?" he asked.

"It's ... weird."

"Do you like it?"

"I don't know. Can we not talk about it?"

He pressed a kiss to the base of her back. "If you really can't stand it, just tell me, and I'll stop."

If a woman didn't want to do anything, he'd leave and find another. This was another reason why he knew Suzy was the one. He had no intention of leaving her, or forcing her. Pixie was content to be whatever she needed him to be. He wanted her, nothing else.

Taking his time, he filled her ass with the fake cock, making sure she was able to take it, and happy for it to stay there.

"Do you want me to stop?"

"No. It feels kind of nice now."

He gripped the base of his cock and pressed inside her tight cunt. With the cock in her ass, her cunt seemed even tighter.

"Oh, fuck," she said.

Holding onto her hips, he pushed his cock in deep, moaning as her cunt repeatedly squeezed around him in little waves and pulses. Closing his eyes, he moaned at the pleasure.

"Touch yourself."

Her hand moved, and he rode her pussy as she brought herself to orgasm. Pixie wasn't in a rush, so each stroke of his cock was long and slow. He took his time, drawing her to a second and third orgasm.

Only when he was sure she was ready did he remove the fake cock from her ass, and push himself inside her gaping hole.

When he did, she screamed his name, not in pain, but in absolute pleasure.

"I'm in your ass, baby. I own every single part of you, and I'm never going to let you go."

She whimpered, submitting to him. He rode her ass, never going too hard or too fast. Her ass had never been used before, and he intended to make her love every second of it.

Making love to her ass, he turned her head, and claimed her lips as he did, owning her. There was no other woman for him. One day he'd have to warn her about the condoms, but that day was not today. He didn't have to worry about her walking away.

With every passing day he was sure of her love for him, and he intended to keep it that way.

****

Teri sat in the diner, rolling her head from side to side as the last of the customers left for the day. Her staff had already gone, and she was so tired.

"Do you think you're getting old?" Leo asked.

"Fuck off. I'm not old." She'd been up since five that very morning, and glancing over at the clock she saw it was past one in the morning. "Tomorrow I'm not opening. It has been a long couple of weeks, and I'm not going to open until I'm ready." She left the table to grab a piece of paper and make a note, warning anyone coming that the diner was closed until at least three for dinner.

"You bad girl," Paul said.

Caleb was sitting at the table with them, and as yet hadn't spoken.

"Are you okay?"

She'd noticed trouble was brewing between Caleb and Kitty, but she'd tried to keep her nose out of it. Sometimes people really didn't want others interfering.

"I'm fine."

"You don't sound fine."

"You can talk to us," Paul said. All playfulness was gone from his voice. When Teri turned back to Leo and Paul, she saw they looked serious. "We're here, and we're ready to hear whatever you have to say."

"It's stupid."

"It's not stupid to you though," Teri said, reaching out to cover his hand with her own. "We're here if you need it."

"We told you about our shit with Stacey," Leo said. "We won't judge."

Leo and Paul came as a package deal in everything. There was no room for choice or manipulation. You took one, you took the both. It was as simple as that. On the same day that James met Cora, Leo and Paul had met Cora's friend Stacey. Everything had been going great, until it was brought to light that Stacey just wanted some fun and fucking rather than an actual commitment. It had broken Teri's heart to see her friends in pain. The Dirty Fuckers MC were her friends, and she cared about them dearly. They were a bunch of horny, sex maniac men, but she loved them. She really did. They meant everything to her. Seeing them settle down and actually be happy was a dream come true to her.

So far, no woman had been willing to take the Leo and Paul sandwich unless it was just for a one-night stand. One day Teri hoped someone would be willing. Until then, she would have to wait, and hold out hope.

"What is it with Kitty? I don't get it. I love her, and she knows I'll do anything for her, but not doing everything is killing me. Life is not supposed to be this way."

"Sweetie," she said. "Have you talked to Kitty?"

"No. You know it's hard to talk to her on a good day." Caleb shook his head. "I can't even be angry with her. That's what sucks the most. I want to be so angry at her, but I can't." Caleb ran erratic fingers through his hair. "Maybe I'm asking too much."

"These things take time."

"How much time? Look at fucking Pixie. The guy was a total asshole, and yet he's away with the woman he loves. We've seen him," Caleb said.

"We can't tell you what to do about Kitty," Leo said. "We can say you're not alone. Look at us two. We want that woman, Caleb. I know I do. It's fun in the beginning having the random partners, fucking whichever pussy anyone wants, but now. I don't want it. I want something else. I want to go home to a woman that will love the two of us, and not be waiting for the next man fantasy to come along."

"We'll get there as well. I know we will," Paul said. "We've just got to believe that it is possible."

"See, Caleb, we're all together." Teri got to her feet, and gripped Caleb's shoulders. She kissed his cheek. "Why don't you go and ask Kitty out on a date? No club members, an actual date. I'll find a place, and then we can take it from there."

Caleb hesitated, and then got to his feet. He kissed her cheek, and she watched him go.

"You're going to help him, but what about us? Do you have a special someone trapped somewhere wanting us?" Paul asked.

She chuckled. "Give me time, and I will attempt to work my magic."

Winking at the two men, she made her way into the kitchen, and stared at the number on the notice board.

There was only one time she had lied to the Dirty Fuckers MC. In the beginning before she knew they were good guys she hadn't told them about her sister. Her sister who was ten years younger than she was, the sweetest girl in the world, and who at the age of twenty-four wanted to connect again.

Teri didn't know what her sister looked like now, but she also didn't want to lose the one person from her family she had left. Letting out a breath, she grabbed the phone, and dialed the number.

"Skylar, hi, it's me. I was wondering if you'd still like to come and live with me for a few months."

She heard her sister's squeal, and of course she would. Skylar had over two months' rent still paid up, but after that, she'd be there.

Teri hung up the phone, and stared out at Leo and Paul.

Maybe, just maybe, she could help them find love soon.

Chapter Eleven

One month later

Pixie rubbed Suzy's back, and he was trying not to freak out himself. This was the third morning in a row that she had rushed to the toilet. She complained about her breasts feeling a little sore, and she seemed to be off certain foods.

Getting back from their vacation, he'd gotten rid of all of the tampered with condoms, replacing them with new ones. He'd prayed and hoped that nothing would happen. However, holding her red hair back from her face, it was starting to be clear that he'd already royally screwed up.

"Do you think I should call James, tell him?" She leaned back, using some tissue to wipe her mouth. "I'm really confused. Yesterday, I felt fine after some water and toast. God, I hate this."

"How about you stay home, and rest, okay?"

She wiped the sweat from her brow. "What about James?"

"I'll go and let him know. I'll be back, and take care of you."

"You'd do that?"

"Of course." He really needed to talk to his brother. He was freaking out, like in a big way right now. He didn't know what to do or what to say.

She was the love of his life, and with several stupid acts he could risk everything.

"You're so good to me."

Kissing her temple, he cursed himself every single name he knew, and then some.

"It's fine. You know me. I can do this."

You're a fucking asshole, loser, and a complete waste of fucking space.

After she brushed her teeth, and she took a shower, he helped her into bed, getting some toast and water for her.

"Here we go, Doctor Pixie to the rescue."

She smiled, and he rested the tray onto her lap.

Grabbing her cell, the e-reader, and the television remote, he handed them all to her, and promised to be back soon.

"Pixie," she said, making him turn. "I know we don't usually talk about our feelings, but I wanted to tell you. I love you."

"You love me?"

"Don't freak out okay. It's nothing something you need to worry about. I won't come stalking you or anything."

He moved back to the bed, and cupped her cheek. "Babe, I've been in love with you for a long fucking time, and that's never going to change."

Pressing a kiss to her lips, Pixie hoped it was going to be enough for her when she found out the truth, even if she had to find out the truth.

Chloe had already left the apartment a few hours before. She worked early for Teri now. Grace took odd hours with baby Joseph. The only reason she worked was because it gave the chance for the club to spoil the little guy.

In the past month a lot had happened. He'd pretty much moved in with Suzy. Richard and Chloe were still doing whatever the hell it was that they were doing. Dane wasn't voted out. None of them wanted to give him a reason to disappear. Ryan was making it difficult, but Lucy made sure that Ryan spent time with his dad.

Teri said she had a surprise for everyone coming next month, which was weird. Usually Teri's surprises included food, or some event she wanted to go to.

Everyone was curious about her little surprise. Right now, Pixie had a feeling he'd put a surprise into Suzy's stomach.

"Fuck, fuck, fuck."

Entering the diner, he saw several of the guys were eating breakfast, but none of them were his brother.

"Where's James?"

"At home." Damon spoke up.

"The clubhouse?" he asked.

"No. He lives with Cora, remember." Damon frowned. "Are you in trouble or something?"

"No. I just really need to see my brother."

Leaving the diner, Pixie climbed on his bike and made his way toward Cora's house. It was a Saturday so Cora wouldn't be at school. Fuck, fuck, he really needed to talk to James.

Riding toward Cora's house, he went over everything he was going to say. The moment Cora opened the door, everything disappeared.

"Pixie, what's up?"

"I really need to speak with James."

"He's in the kitchen."

Entering the room, James's smile disappeared. "What did you do?"

"You know that just by looking at him?" Cora asked.

"He's my brother. I know when he's fucked up, when he needs help, or when he's smug about something. Right now, my brother has his 'fucked up, help me' face." James took a sip of his coffee. "Spill."

"It really needs to be in private."

Cora snorted.

"Whatever you've got to say has to be said in front of her. She may be able to help whatever you've done."

"Actually if it's cheating, murder, or anything else, count me out."

"Why the fuck would you say cheating?" Pixie asked.

"You're a guy supposedly going steady with a friend. I've also had every single member tell me how you can't even go steady with anyone."

"I would never cheat on Suzy. I fucking love her."

Cora grinned, clapped her hands, and held her hand out. "Pay up."

Pixie watched as James pulled out a hundred dollars and handed them to Cora. "What the fuck? You're betting on me now?"

"Damon called to let us know you were on your way here, which is why we had time to get changed, and to debate what Pixie would need from us this morning," Cora said.

"She took a bet, saying that you were going to tell us you were in love with Suzy. I said not."

"Look, whatever. The love I feel for Suzy is not why I'm here."

"Give me back my money," James said, smirking.

"I said he'd say the words. Not that it was going to be the reason he was here," Cora said. "You lost, fair and square."

James laughed, turning back to him. "What's wrong, brother?"

Pixie took a seat. "You can't tell Suzy," he said, looking at Cora.

"Fine, fine."

"How do I start? I'll just go with it. Suzy doesn't take birth control pills. She doesn't like them, and has never needed them. I told her I'd take care of the protection. Anyway, one day I completely forgot, and I had sex without the condom. I don't think she realized it, but I did."

"Did you pull out?"

"No."

"Did you realize after the event?" James asked, suddenly looking serious.

"I realized during, but I suddenly realized that if I finished inside, I might find another way to keep her."

"Why don't you tell Suzy the mistake you made?"

Pixie's nerves were completely shattered. "To make sure I got her pregnant I then proceeded to take a needle, and pierce every single condom I owned within its packet."

Cora gasped, and his shame continued.

"Without her knowing. I've been making love to Suzy, and the condoms have all been compromised."

James didn't say anything. "Go on. I know you, Pixie, you're not finished."

"Um, when I truly saw what the fuck I was doing, and how much of a stupid idiot I was being, I replaced them all. Just tossed them out, and got new."

"Okay…"

"Three days in a row, Suzy has been vomiting, her tits are tender, and her stomach revolts against certain food. Before you ask, I've already done an internet search, and yeah, all other signs point to the fact she's pregnant. I've got a test at the club, which I bought at the same time." He finished. "What do I do?"

Silence fell around the kitchen. He stared at his brother, and then at Cora. They both simply looked at him.

"You're my big brother. You're supposed to help me out here. Tell me what to do, how to make it better?"

James didn't say a word for several moments,

simply staring at him. "I warned you that your actions would soon have consequences, Pixie. I can't help you with this one. This is all on you."

Pixie's stomach clenched. "I've got to tell her the truth."

"Yes. You have."

He dropped his head. Tears were so close to the surface, but he didn't let them come out.

"I'm sorry," he said.

"What for?"

"For letting you down. I didn't think of anything other than finally having a reason to keep Suzy to myself."

"She may not be angry," James said.

"She will be. I only hope I have what it takes to win her back." Pixie stood up, and let out a breath. "I finally see what you and Drake do. When you find that woman, you really will do stupid shit to keep them."

****

Suzy couldn't believe what she was hearing. She didn't want to believe it, but Pixie was telling the truth. He held a pregnancy test, and told her the truth of how he intended to manipulate her into keeping her.

Pregnant.

The sickness.

The soreness.

The lack of appetite. She didn't want to believe it, yet she knew it was true.

Storming toward him, she took the test out of his hands, and went to the bathroom. She wanted to know the answer before she kicked him out. He'd purposefully set about making her pregnant, and now she was going to have deal with it.

Reading through the instructions, she followed them exactly.

"Baby, I'm not going to go anywhere." Pixie's voice called through the door, and she didn't want to hear him right now. She was so angry.

"You broke the condoms on purpose, or you just forgot them."

"I wanted you. I didn't think about anything else but you."

"You think this is supposed to be romantic?" she asked.

"I love you, I want you. No one else. I wasn't really thinking about anything else."

"A baby is a living breathing person, Pixie. It's not something you put in a box or push to one side thinking 'oops, I made a mistake'." Opening the bathroom door, she glared at him. "I had a right to make a decision on children."

"You love me."

"And that is what makes this hurt so much. I love you, Pixie, and instead of trusting in me, in us, you set about making sure I didn't have a choice."

"I'm sorry."

She squeezed her hands into fists, and growled. "I don't want to hear it. There I've said it. Your sorry, your apologies is not going to make everything better. It's only going to make everything worse."

The alarm went off, and she went to the sink where she'd put the test. Her entire world spun on its axis, and turned right over.

Pregnant.

She was pregnant with Pixie's child.

"Get out!"

"Baby."

"Get out. Get out."

"We need to talk about this."

"Right now I want to kill you. I don't want to talk

about this. I want you to get out. I want you to leave." She threw the test at him, and she was surprised that he caught it. "Get out. I don't want to talk to you right now."

"Suzy, I love you."

She paused. "Then you should have thought about that before you decided to take our future into your own hands."

Pushing him out of the apartment, she slammed the door closed, and then slid down it. What the hell was she going to do? Her hands were shaking with the rage at what he'd done. She hadn't been lying this morning when she told him she loved him. She did love him, loved him so much.

Tears spilled from her eyes, rushing down her cheeks, and spilling into her lap.

She loved him so completely, and yet he hadn't had any faith in her, in this.

Time passed, and she finally got onto the sofa. Fluffy came to curl up against her. He'd stayed well away from their fighting. Chloe finally arrived, and once she removed her jacket, she was there, on the sofa.

"I've heard," Chloe said.

"I bet everyone heard. They heard what an idiot I've been."

"No. Pixie, he told everyone what he did. The club, they're disappointed in him. He wanted them to know that he'd fucked up, and that he was going to do whatever it took to make things right."

"It doesn't matter," Suzy said.

"Why?"

"I don't know."

"What are you thinking?" Chloe asked.

"I don't know. I don't know what I'm thinking. I don't know what I feel. I'm torn about everything." Pixie had taken her choice out of getting pregnant, and she didn't know what to do or to even think about that. She loved him, and he said that he loved her.

"Do you want me to kick his ass?"

Suzy laughed. "No. I'll kick it when I think the time is right."

"So you're going to see him again."

"I'm not going to stop seeing him, Chloe. He's the father of my child. That was weird."

"Totally. Wow, you're going to have a baby. Pixie's baby. I never thought I'd see the day that he'd settle down, and yet he's going to do it with you."

"Do you really think he loves me, or do you think he was just saying that because he knew what he'd done?" Suzy nibbled her lip, hoping her fears weren't right.

"He loves you, Suzy. I've seen a change in him, and it wasn't overnight either. I've noticed it for the past year, even before that. He wanted you, and he's worked hard to try and get you. How do you feel?"

"Even as it hurts right now with what he's done, I miss him." She wiped the tears from her eyes. "What do I do about my job?"

"I don't know. James won't take sides. I bet he's really pissed right now at his brother."

"I don't want him to get in trouble," Suzy said.

"He won't. James probably already knows. All the guys go to him for problems." Chloe pushed her hair out of her face.

"I haven't asked you how you're doing."

"I'm not the one that has turned up pregnant. That is certainly a new one, right."

"Yeah. How are you and Richard?"

"Difficult. I never expected it to be hard, but then I should have known it wouldn't be easy."

Closing her eyes, they settled into the sofa.

"Shall I order takeout?" Chloe asked.

"Please."

****

The following day Suzy stood in James's office after avoiding seeing Pixie. She saw the pity in several of the club members' eyes, and it made her feel sick. This was what she had hoped to avoid, yet it wasn't even down to the fact he dumped her.

"I'm not going to let you quit," James said.

"You know the truth?"

"I was the one that told him to tell you the truth. Think about it, Suzy, he could have just said a condom broke. No matter how much you're hurting right now, he did tell you the truth."

She nodded. "I wasn't asking if I could quit. I just wanted to make sure I still had a job. Pixie is your brother."

"I know my brother very well. I know he's not the easiest man to get along with. Damn, he's not even the easiest man to like." James stopped. "But with you I saw him change. He'll still be my asshole little brother, but I finally got to see the true Pixie. The guy he keeps on hiding."

Tears filled her eyes and spilled down her face. "I don't know what to do."

"Don't do anything. Just know that we all care about you, and about Pixie. I truly hope someday you can find it in your heart to forgive him." James stood and rounded the desk. He held his arms open. "This is not a come on, or anything. I just want to give the woman, the mother of my future niece or nephew, a hug."

She laughed, and walked into his arms. She gave him a quick squeeze, and stepped back. Cora came in, and smiled. "Better not be stealing my man."

"I wouldn't." She had one of her own. One that she was really pissed at.

"We're all having dinner at the diner if you'd like to join us. Pixie will be there before you ask," Cora said.

"I don't know."

"You're carrying his baby. The next generation of Dirty Fuckers. We all know. May as well get used to the fact that you're now part of the club."

"Then I'll come to dinner," she said.

There was no point running from the club. She needed them, and even though she was pissed at Pixie right now, she wasn't going to stop him from seeing their child. She probably wouldn't even be mad for very long. At the moment, she was just hurt, and she needed to deal with it.

Chapter Twelve

The days went by, and Pixie refused to pretend nothing was going on. When Suzy was around, he still went to see her. Conversation was a little awkward for her, but he refused to be put off. He'd fucked up, and he knew it. There was nothing he could do to change what was going on. The last thing he was going to do was abandon the woman he loved.

So while she worked, he studied her, watching for any signs that the pregnancy was wearing on her.

Of course he spoke to her. He rarely was able to be quiet.

"You look more beautiful each day. I wonder if that is the whole glow thing from the pregnancy."

Nothing. She kept on working.

"I know I fucked up. I really hope you can forgive me. I was also looking for places to live."

She looked up then. "Why?"

"Our kid can't be stuck in an apartment. At first I thought we could live here. We've got a pretty large yard out back, but then I figured that wouldn't be good enough for our kid, so I'm thinking a house. Luck would have it, there's a house for sale next to Cora. Not the old man's place, but a couple who seem to have split. I didn't get the details."

"I'm not moving in with you."

"You can't keep me out of your life, Suzy. I love you."

"You messed with condoms. You damaged them so I would get pregnant."

"Can't you see that as romantic?"

She shook her head. "Pixie, you can't do romance. You do fucking."

"What about our vacation? I did a lot of

romance."

"Fucking."

"We made love," he said.

"I really need to work, and I can't do my job if I'm arguing with you."

He was silent for several minutes as he stared at her. She looked so beautiful, and even though she hadn't really spoken to him for a few days, he knew she still loved him. Also, he talked with Kitty, and she told him the reason it can hurt so much is the fact you loved them so much. So, in theory, Suzy was pissed because she loved him too much.

"I'm going to leave you in peace, but the way I saw it as being romantic is the fact that I didn't know how else to keep you."

"Pixie?"

"No, let me speak. I've never loved a woman. I've never cared about a woman. Then you come along, and I can't stop thinking about you. All I want to know is if you're okay, and it twists me up inside to think someone could take you away from me. It was wrong, and I have an entirely fucked up reasoning, but I can promise you, everything I did, it was out of love." Running fingers through his hair, he stared into her eyes. "I can't stop thinking about you. I love you that much, and I don't know if I'm even good enough to keep you, but I know I never want to let you go."

"You hurt me."

"Then let me prove to you that I can be the guy you need. I can give you the romance. Please, Suzy, I don't want to lose my shot with you."

She bit her lip and stared down at her paperwork. "Okay."

"Excellent. Prepare to be romanced."

He left the room, and without stopping, he got on

his bike, and rode out of the clubhouse. Romance was not something he was good at. He had just crooked his finger, women had fallen at his feet, giving him whatever his heart desired.

You've got this.

Over the next two weeks, Pixie did everything he could find in romance books. Seriously, he read romance books, and not the nice sweet romance kind. He went hard core erotica. It was all the rage now, and he intended to use those authors to find out the best way to show his woman, he loved her.

Flowers and chocolates were the easiest.

Next he went with jewelry, which didn't bode well with him. Suzy wasn't the jewelry kind of woman. After that, he organized dates. Well, in order to help him not screw up, he double dated her.

One night he went with James and Cora. His brother stopped him from putting his foot in it, and ruining everything. He hated it when men looked toward Suzy, and he wanted to stake his claim. His double date with Drake and Grace didn't go so well either. He took her to the movies, and he ended up yelling at the assholes who kept interrupting the movie. Suzy asked him to stop, but he didn't. In the end, he was the one that got kicked out for threatening bodily harm. *Assholes!* The date with Sharon and Thomas went better. They went to the zoo, which was a fucked up place to have a date, but it worked. Suzy loved the day, and Pixie believed he was making real progress.

Visits and sleepovers at her house had ceased. During the day he was able to stay close to the club as she worked nonstop for James. The nights were the hardest for him. Sleeping alone was next to impossible. He missed curling around his woman, and loving her.

About three weeks' worth of romance, Pixie sat

in the diner with Teri enjoying a coffee. He'd dropped Suzy back at her apartment, and come to the diner.

"You're looking down in the dumps," Teri said, straddling a chair.

"Not exactly in a good mood."

"Why not?"

"Life, relationships, I suck at them."

She pushed some hair out of her face, staring at him. "You really do love Suzy."

"Yeah, hasn't anyone been paying attention? She's my fucking life, and I'm the one that blew it." He rubbed his eyes.

"It was a shitty thing that you did."

"You don't think I know that. If I could take it back, I would, but I would never change the time I had with Suzy."

"She hasn't cut you out of her life."

"I know." He pulled the black velvet box out of his pocket.

"Holy shit."

"Do you think she'll even accept this?" He flipped it open. "I bought it the night before she was sick again. I was going to propose over breakfast. Instead, I started to get really scared that I'd been caught out."

Teri took the box, opening it up. "You're really serious."

"Yeah. I just wish Suzy could forgive me."

"How about I close the diner tomorrow night? You bring her here, have a romantic meal, and propose. Lay all of your cards on the table. I think she'd surprise you."

"You do?"

"Suzy is hurt, and I'm not justifying what you did. I think it was really shitty, but I also know you love her. You really do, and she loves you. There's no changing that." She smiled at him. "I think you'll make a pretty good dad."

"You think so."

"The club will make sure of it."

"You're the best, Teri. Really."

"I try."

****

Suzy glanced over at Teri wondering what was going on. Pixie called her to get ready for dinner, and without giving her a chance to decline, he hung up.

"Where is he?" she asked.

"Pixie has a little surprise for you. I think you'll be surprised, and I hope you can find it in your heart to forgive him."

"Do you think me being pissed is wrong?"

"No, absolutely not. You have a right to be pissed. Pixie, he went about everything the wrong way. Even I'm pissed at him, but I've noticed a change in the both of you. You love him, Suzy. You can't tell me these past few weeks have been easy."

"They haven't been easy."

"They've not been easy for Pixie either. I only hope you can both find some happiness together."

Once they were at the diner, Suzy noticed it was dark.

"I'm not going on. Everything is ready," Teri said.

Climbing out of the car, Suzy made her way into the diner. There at a single table in the center was Pixie. He wore a tuxedo, and he lit two candles.

"Hello, beautiful."

"Pixie," she said.

"I wish I could have come and got you myself, but I had strict instructions on what to do. Please, would you take a seat?"

She moved toward the seat he'd pulled out, and lowered herself down. "This is beautiful."

"Only the best for my girl."

He poured out some water, and she noticed he took water as well.

"You did all of this?"

"With Teri's help. Actually, it was her idea."

"She really is something."

He nodded, finally taking a seat. She stared across the table, her heart racing.

"I've missed you," she said, the words spilling from her lips. "I like having you to cuddle up to."

Pixie took her hand.

"Everything just got screwed up," she said.

"No. *I* screwed up, and you had a right to be pissed. I would have been pissed. I miss you. How is everything?"

She pressed a hand to her stomach. "Fine. I'm going to see the doctor in two days. I should have made an appointment sooner, but with everything that happened, I kind of forgot."

"I want to be there."

"I'd like that."

Silence fell between them.

"Oh, fuck this." He got out of his chair and down on one knee. "Suzy, I fucked up. I really did, and I wanted this to be an entire romantic evening, where everything was built up, and I showed you how I can be the perfect guy for you, but the truth is, I can't. I'm me. I can promise you that my entire life will be devoted to you, and to the children we have. I bought this before I even suspected you were pregnant." He lifted the lid on the black velvet box. "Suzy, will you do me the honor of becoming my wife? I know. Marrying an asshole isn't exactly a good pitch, but I know I can make you happy."

He kept on talking about how he'd love and protect her. Tears filling her eyes, she silenced him with a kiss.

Cupping his face, she pulled away, and smiled. "Yes."

"Yes?"

"You want to marry me, right? That's why you got the ring?"

"Hell yeah, I just thought I'd have to convince you of it some more." He slid the ring on her finger. "Don't want you changing your mind."

She stared down at the ring, smiling. "I wouldn't change my mind. It's beautiful."

"Do you forgive me?" He placed his hand on her stomach.

Covering his hand with her on, she smiled. "I was hurt, Pixie. Hurt, scared, excited, nervous. I never thought I'd have kids, and now I am."

"I'll look after you. I'll take care of you. I'll always take care of you."

"I love you, Pixie. I really do, and I know that even if we do encounter some bumps in the road, that love is never going to change." She cupped his cheek. "I forgive you, Pixie."

He leaned in close, and kissed her. "Let's eat so I can take you home, and we can have a good night's sleep."

"Just to sleep?"

"Fuck yeah, I haven't slept any in the last three weeks. I'm fucking exhausted."

Suzy giggled, holding Pixie close. Yes, he was an asshole but he was her asshole, and she wouldn't have him any other way. The next time though, she was going to be the one protecting the condoms.

****

Teri watched as the club sat around several tables, checking things off for the wedding. As part of his act of contrition Pixie was organizing the wedding. He was going to give Suzy the dream wedding, the church, the tuxedos, the flowers, the cake, all of it. Teri loved watching the club, and seeing the way they were all growing. Staring at Leo and Paul, she wanted to help them. They clearly needed someone, and soon.

Checking her watch, she kept on looking outside waiting for her sister. She hadn't told any of the club that her sister was on her way to see her. Well, she'd told them that she had someone visiting, not necessarily her sister.

Just as Teri looked up, she noticed a cab pulled outside of the diner. She noticed Skylar's raven hair first, then her pale skin, finally her full figure. There were a lot of years between them, but Teri knew Skylar was very nervous about her curves. Their mother, if someone wanted to even call the woman that, would make Skylar's life a nightmare. Teri remembered coming home to find Skylar being forced to exercise. It wasn't just a healthy exercise either. Their mother had her doing it for four hours, and even sent her to bed without food.

Leaving the diner, she stood watching her sister.

"Sky," she said.

Her sister turned toward her, and smiled. It was the smile that got Teri most of all. Skylar was the nicest person Teri had ever known. She had lost touch with her, and now she had the chance to make everything right.

"Teri," Sky said.

Rushing toward each other, they embraced, hugging each other hard.

"It has been too long," Teri said.

"I'm so glad you called. I was worried you wouldn't want to see me again."

"Always." Pulling away, Teri pushed her hair off her face. "Come on, there's some people I want you to meet." Taking her hand, she entered the diner, and smiled at the men, who were staring curiously at the two of them. "Everyone, this is my sister, Skylar. Skylar, this is everyone from the Dirty Fuckers MC."

Skylar held her hand up and waved. "Hello."

Teri looked at Leo and Paul. She wanted to jump up and down in victory. Her sister had a lot of issues, and she knew the two men held the power to help her. Maybe, just maybe, all three could be what they were looking for.

Epilogue

Six months later

Lying in the bath against Pixie's chest, Suzy giggled as he traced over her swollen stomach.

"My kid is not being called Randy."

"How about Burt?" she asked, glancing up.

"We don't even know if it's a boy or girl. What about Sienna? I like that name for a girl."

"I like that name as well."

He ran his fingers over her stomach, marveling at how his son or daughter kicked out. "They're going to be fighters, either of them."

Staring down into Suzy's smiling face, Pixie knew his world was complete.

"The baby is due in like two months, and we've just found this house. We're going to need to fully furnish it."

"The guys are going to help tomorrow. Consider it an extended wedding gift."

She lifted her hand out of the water, showing off her wedding band. "I sometimes forget we're married."

"What surprised me was finding out that James and Cora are now married. Neither of them gave anyone any warning."

"Sucks. I'd have liked to have watched those two get married," Suzy said.

He took hold of her hand, locking their fingers together. "They wouldn't even consider renewing our vows when we got married."

"My wedding day was perfect." She glanced back up at him. "Thank you."

"Anything for you. Forever and for always."

"Such a charmer."

He cupped her face and pressed a kiss to her lips.

What a difference six months had made. He was married. Skylar had moved in with Chloe, and had even made them their wedding cake. Pixie hadn't known Teri had a sister let alone one that baked. The whole club was excited to meet her. She was the complete opposite of Teri though, shy and nervous. Still the same lovable personality, just hard to talk with at times.

"Do you know who sent Skylar those roses?" he asked.

"Leo and Paul. I heard the two of them while they placed their order. I think they have a soft spot for her. She's a lovely person. I adore her."

"You don't miss being at the apartment? Keeping me away."

"I married you, Pixie, so I could have a reason to spend more time with you." She went to her knees, and he helped her as her stomach got in her way. "I'm a tank."

"A beautiful tank."

"Will you still love me with all my stretch marks?" she asked, pouting.

"I will love you more because of them." He kissed her neck, then moved down to her breasts. "As each day goes by, I find myself loving you more and more. I promised to devote my life to yours, and I will every single day." Sinking his fingers into her hair, he tugged her down for a kiss. "Now, show your husband how much you love him."

It took all night, but by the end of it, Pixie lay with Suzy in his arms, sated, and content. The next fifty years were going to be the best of his life.

The End

EVERNIGHT PUBLISHING ®

www.evernightpublishing.com

Printed in Great Britain
by Amazon

23811238R00096